John Creasey – Master Storyteller

Born in Surrey, England in 1908 into a poor family in which there were nine children, John Creasey grew up to be a true master story teller and international sensation. His more than 600 crime, mystery and thriller titles have now sold 80 million copies in 25 languages. These include many popular series such as *Gideon of Scotland Yard, The Toff, Dr Palfrey* and *The Baron*.

Creasy wrote under many pseudonyms, explaining that booksellers had complained he totally dominated the 'C' section in stores. They included:

Gordon Ashe, M E Cooke, Norman Deane, Robert Caine Frazer, Patrick Gill, Michael Halliday, Charles Hogarth, Brian Hope, Colin Hughes, Kyle Hunt, Abel Mann, Peter Manton, J J Marric, Richard Martin, Rodney Mattheson, Anthony Morton and Jeremy York.

Never one to sit still, Creasey had a strong social conscience, and stood for Parliament several times, along with founding the One Party Alliance which promoted the idea of government by a coalition of the best minds from across the political spectrum.

He also founded the British Crime Writers' Association, which to this day celebrates outstanding crime writing. The Mystery Writers of America bestowed upon him the Edgar Award for best novel and then in 1969 the ultimate Grand Master Award. John Creasey's stories are as compelling today as ever.

THE TOFF SERIES

A Bundle for the Toff
A Doll for the Toff
A Knife for the Toff
A Mask for the Toff
A Rocket for the Toff
A Score for the Toff
Accuse the Toff
Break the Toff
Call the Toff
Double for the Toff
Feathers for the Toff
Follow the Toff
Fool the Toff
Hammer the Toff
Here Comes the Toff
Hunt the Toff
Introducing the Toff
Kill the Toff
Leave It to the Toff
Kiss the Toff
Model for the Toff
Poison for the Toff
Salute the Toff
Stars for the Toff
Terror for the Toff
The Kidnapped Child
The Toff Among the Millions
The Toff and Old Harry
The Toff and the Crooked Copper

The Toff and the Deadly Parson
The Toff and the Deep Blue Sea
The Toff and the Fallen Angels
The Toff and the Golden Boy
The Toff and the Great Illusion
The Toff and the Lady
The Toff and the Runaway Bride
The Toff and the Sleepy Cowboy
The Toff and the Spider
The Toff and the Stolen Tresses
The Toff and the Toughs
The Toff and the Terrified Taxman
The Toff and the Trip-Trip-Triplets
The Toff at Butlins
The Toff at the Fair
The Toff Breaks In
The Toff Goes On
The Toff Goes to Market
The Toff in New York
The Toff in Town
The Toff in Wax
The Toff Is Back
The Toff on Board
The Toff on Fire
The Toff Proceeds
The Toff Steps Out
The Toff Takes Shares
Vote for the Toff

Murder Out of the Past (short stories)
The Toff on the Trail (short stories)

The Toff in New York
John Creasey

Copyright © 1956 John Creasey; 2009 House of Stratus

All rights reserved. No part of this publication may be reproduced, stored in a retrieval system, or transmitted, in any form, or by any means (electronic, mechanical, photocopying, recording, or otherwise), without the prior permission of the publisher. Any person who does any unauthorised act in relation to this publication may be liable to criminal prosecution and civil claims for damages.

The right of John Creasey to be identified as the author of this work has been asserted.

This edition published in 2009 by House of Stratus, an imprint of Stratus Books Ltd., 21 Beeching Park, Kelly Bray, Cornwall, PL17 8QS, UK.

www.houseofstratus.com

Typeset, printed and bound by House of Stratus.

A catalogue record for this book is available from the British Library and the Library of Congress.

ISBN 07551-1760-3
EAN 978-07551-1760-4

This book is sold subject to the condition that it shall not be lent, resold, hired out, or otherwise circulated without the publisher's express prior consent in any form of binding, or cover, other than the original as herein published and without a similar condition being imposed on any subsequent purchaser, or bona fide possessor.

This is a fictional work and all characters are drawn from the author's imagination. Any resemblance or similarities to persons either living or dead are entirely coincidental.

1

SWEET INNOCENCE

THE girl leaned close to the window of the stratocruiser, peering down on wonderland.

A few minutes ago, there had been the darkness of the Atlantic and, in the distance, single lights or tiny clusters. The fair-haired young man with the magnificent smile had told her that they were over Long Island. Now, although he sat beside her, he had the sense to keep quiet.

Everyone was quiet; even the hardened travellers, the old and young soaks, the flinty-hearted and the foolish, New York spread out beneath them, and from the air and after dark New York was the wonderland of the modern world.

The girl was seeing it for the first time.

She was round-eyed and marvelling, which was the proper reaction, and everyone approved. She seemed to hold her breath. Gradually, the lights drew nearer. White, yellow, red, green, blue - so many colours that it looked as if the rainbow had been broken into tiny pieces and scattered down there, catching radiance from the stars. There were long, straight lines of light, vanishing into the illimitable distance of darkness. There were short stretches of light. There were pools of it. There were clusters. There were fairy lights stretched across dark voids. From up here, all of these were unaccountable, part of a mystery that was almost a miracle.

The girl, round-eyed as if in dewy innocence and wonder, dropped back into her seat, and let out a long, long sigh. She closed her eyes for a moment, as if the picture of the scene below had somehow to be shut out, so that she could come back to the real world. Then, she opened her eyes and turned to look at her companion. He was not only fair-haired but handsome in a rugged way, a man whose blue eyes seemed to tell of the great open spaces, whose square, jutting chin suggested both character and stubbornness alike; a young maid's dream of a heroic young man.

"Like it?" he asked, and there was a proprietorial air about his manner, as if he had taken out an option on the view, and hoped to sell it to her.

"It's - quite wonderful," she said.

"Yes, isn't it?" he agreed, with airy nonchalance.

He had an accent which wasn't quite English and wasn't quite American and yet certainly wasn't Canadian. His large, firm hand rested for a moment on the girl's arm.

"Like me to pick out a few places for you?" he suggested.

"Yes - yes, please."

The girl leaned closer to the window, and the young man had to press against her, but that wasn't really embarrassing. He rested one hand on her left shoulder, and his cheek was very close to hers. His right hand pointed. The aircraft was circling and losing height, but it was obvious that the young man knew this view backwards and probably upside down.

"See that long stretch of lights, wanders off to the left a bit - that's Broadway. See that place where the lights seem twice as bright as anywhere else? That's Times Square. See that string of lights across the dark stretch - that's the George Washington Bridge, spanning the Hudson River." He didn't sound the least bit excited, just went on and on. "Queensborough Bridge - Triborough Bridge - Bronx - Brooklyn - the Empire State Building, Woolworth's Building, Atyeo Building, Chrysler, Uno, Central Park, 5th Avenue" - it was a never-ending stream, and all the time the young man's hand was firm on the girl's shoulder and his cheek drew closer to hers; so close, that once or twice she felt the roughness of his fair stubble.

Then came the stewardess; no smoking, fasten belts, hustle and bustle, some slight tension on the part of many passengers, a woman who began to talk in a high-pitched voice and wouldn't stop, glucose and barley sugar, bump, bump, bump.

"Here we are," said the fair-haired young man. "Idle-wild! By George, it's good to be back!" He was unfastening his belt, for the aircraft was taxing now. The only lights appeared to be at the airport control tower and along the edges of the landing-strips and, in the distance, the headlights of cars. "I suppose you're being met."

"Oh, yes," the girl told him; "my brother will be here."

"That's fine," said the fair-haired young man, "but if you should need anything, you'll let me know, won't you?"

"It's very kind of you, but I'm sure I won't."

He smiled.

She smiled.

The door was opened, the line of passengers began the trek along the gangway towards the steps and the airfield. Most of them had a word of thanks for the stewardesses, some had handshakes. Voices seemed to float out of the aircraft into the cool night, and then to fade away. The girl had only a small bag and some magazines, and the young man, with a brief-case and oddments, made no attempt to help her. They walked together towards the airport building, customs, porters, the waiting, welcoming crowd. Most of the passengers seemed to have someone to meet them. A little group of men carrying cameras gathered at one spot. Suddenly the cameras clicked and the flashlights dazzled, as a little, insignificant man with a face rather like a monkey was greeted. He posed, impatiently. No one on board the aircraft had even suspected that he was distinguished. He was, in fact, a boxing promoter.

The young man elbowed the photographers aside, so as to clear a path for the girl.

"Thank you," she said again.

Now, it was all over. The customs officers were waiting, for the luggage had been brought in very quickly. The girl looked round for her brother, but did not see him. Everyone else seemed to have someone to wave to, but not she or the young man. He was brisk and businesslike now, as if he had more to do than worry about a round-eyed sweetie in the early twenties, filled, it seemed, with the wonder of young innocence.

Her passport was studied and solemnly stamped.

Clearance labels were stuck on her cases.

She was accepted into this New World.

She went into the big hall, and kept looking round, anxiously. There seemed to be hundreds of people, obviously of many nationalities, most of them sitting quietly and patiently, a few noisy and one or two angry about no understandable thing. The only accent which did not sound high above the rest was American.

The girl left her luggage, and walked about. The building was much larger than she had expected, and now she realised that there were thousands of people here; but she did not see her brother. It was a little after ten o'clock, and the plane had arrived half an hour late, so it wasn't because she was early. She walked, solitary, gracefully, worriedly. She wore a small black-and-white check suit, beautifully simple, and a little black hat on shiny dark hair, white blouse, black shoes. Her figure would probably make a man dream as soon as he realised how cunningly it was adorned. She wasn't really a beauty, but undoubtedly she caught the eye. Her eyes were blue and her nose a little broad and tip-tilted and her mouth rather wide. Her profile was the nicest thing about her, and the way she walked was superb. A lot of people noticed that, and among these was a tall, dark man who had come off the aircraft - and who, in fact, had observed her closely most of the way across.

He wore one of those suits which had obviously come

from Savile Row, he had an air with him, and was too handsome to be true. He did not follow the girl, but whenever she came back into the main hall, he watched her. The fair-haired young man was very busy about this and that and things, and no longer seemed to notice her. They were the only three stratocruiser passengers left in the hall when, half an hour after their luggage had been cleared, the young man walked smartly towards the door. Suddenly he stopped, as if startled at finding the girl still here.

He smiled, warmly.

"Hallo, are you still around?" He managed to make that silly remark sound intelligent.

"Yes," she said; for what else could she? "My brother" she broke off. "I'm just going to telephone his hotel."

"Great Scott! hasn't he come?"

"No," she confessed, and for a moment sounded woe-begone.

The tall, dark man was in earshot, and this gem of bright conversation appeared to afford him some amusement, although when he smiled he looked away from the couple. They stood together, the girl more than a little forlorn now, although there was a stubborn glint in her eyes; and the fair-haired young man giving an excellent impression of a gallant who did not want to force his attentions too far.

"Well," he said, "let's go and call him, shall we? What hotel is he at?"

"The Arden-Astoria," said the girl.

If this startled or impressed the young man, he concealed it well, and as they turned towards a row of telephone booths, he said:

"He couldn't have mixed up the times of the planes, I suppose?"

"I don't know."

"What a shame it is," said the fair-haired young man.

Now, the tall, dark man turned away sharply, as if anxious

to make sure that they could not see how this exchange amused him. There was a certain awkwardness, almost a sense of constraint, between the younger couple.

They reached the telephones, and the young man put the call through for her. She asked for Mr. Wilfred Hall and, after a while, was told that he was out. Slowly, worried, she put back the receiver.

The 'boy' gave a sudden, dashing smile, and burst out:

"Look here, can I see you to the hotel? My time's my own, and I'd be glad to."

"You're very good . . ."

"Be no trouble at all," he declared, and now that the ice was really broken, he gave a little laugh which made it obvious that being her escort would give him a lot of pleasure. "I've a car outside - a friend is waiting for me."

"Well," the girl said, "I ought to wait a bit longer for Wilf."

"I'm not so sure," said the young man, with great earnestness. "If he's as late as this - getting on for an hour - I doubt if he'll turn up. But I'll tell you what, let's give him another half-hour, and then drive into New York. Could have been delayed: traffic out to Idlewild gets terribly thick sometimes. What night is it?"

"Saturday."

"Ah, yes, Saturday over the Queensborough Bridge can take an hour. Would you care for a cup of coffee?"

"No, thanks," Wilfred Hall's sister said, "and I don't like the idea of keeping your friend waiting."

"Oh, he won't mind. Let's go and have a word with him," suggested the young man and then, for the first time since he had smiled so brightly, he appeared to hesitate. "I'd like to introduce you, but - well, I'm Brian Conway."

So naive.

"I'm Valerie Hall."

"Glad to know you, Miss Hall!" The young man sounded as if all was now wonderful in a perfect world. He took her elbow and they walked towards the exit and the great car-park. The tall, dark-haired man followed at a distance, which he reduced as they stepped into the open air. Out here there was little light, and he could see them both as silhouettes, and could hear their voices. "I ought to warn you," Brian Conway went on to Valerie, "my friend is a bit of a rough diamond."

"Is he?"

"Yes, but don't let it worry you," said Conway, breezily "he has been living rough for a long time, prospecting up in Canada. Doesn't really like the highlights of civilisation - you can imagine what it's like when you've been living out in the sticks for years, can't you?"

"Er - yes," said Valerie Hall, dubiously.

"He's a great chap though," enthused Conway, "and do I owe him plenty!"

"Really?" Valerie showed a proper interest.

Conway laughed; a deep, satisfied, happy sound. He squeezed Valerie's arm, but did not attempt to explain this sudden change of mood. Instead, he looked round. He did not see the tall, dark-haired man, who had taken shelter behind two cars. The night was very dark, and they seemed to be walking among thousands of cars, all enormous.

"Between you and me," Conway said at last, "I owe Mike Halloran the better part of a million pounds. How's that? Anyone else would have cut me out - or at most paid me back my original stake, but not Mike. Fifty-fifty we'd agreed, in a verbal agreement only, and his word proved to be as good as his bond. If you ever want proof of a thing like that, a million pounds is pretty good!"

"I should think it is," agreed Valerie, solemnly.

They walked between two more rows of cars, and then Conway exclaimed: "There he is!" A light was on in one car where a man sat reading a newspaper. He looked up as they approached, and put his newspaper down. He didn't attempt to open the door; Conway did that. Then he introduced one Mike Halloran, and Valerie Hall found herself looking into the deep-set eyes of a man with a face so craggy that it might have been carved out of rock which had turned the edge of the sculptor's chisel. There was nothing even slightly smooth about it. If the weather of a thousand years had been let loose on that countenance and by a process of erosion made very few alterations on the original, no one would have been surprised. He did not so much need a shave as look as if there were parts of his chin and cheeks so deeply chiselled that no razor could get at the chasms. Yet ostensibly he was clean-shaven. His eyes were buried so deep that it was hard to be sure of their colour but easy to see that they were very bright.

"Why, ma'am," said Mike Halloran, "I'm right glad to know you."

He put out a hand.

Valerie entrusted hers. Halloran took it, and gripped - and when she was on the point of wincing he stopped, as if realising that in his grasp was some precious and perhaps even breakable thing. He let her fingers go.

"Real glad," he said, in a granite-hard voice.

"Mike, I've promised to wait for half an hour to see if her brother arrives," Conway said, "and if he doesn't, we'll run her to her hotel - are you staying at the Arden-Astoria hotel, Miss Hall?"

"Oh, yes," Valerie said; "I don't know whether it's very central."

She looked hopeful.

"Arden-Astoria," said Halloran, after a long pause; "can't say I've ever heard tell of the place."

Conway chuckled, as if deeply amused.

"Mike, you ought to go and live in a cave where the uranium is!" he said. "Believe it or not, Miss Hall, Mike spent five years prospecting for uranium before he struck it rich, and half that time he slept in the open. Why, one winter he actually lived in a cave."

Halloran grinned; and showed that he had yellow but strong-looking teeth.

"It was me or the grizzly," he declared, "and I never did like grizzlies all that much."

Valerie found herself laughing.

Brian Conway said: "Shake yourself up for a while, Mike; come and have a cup of coffee while we're waiting with Miss Hall. Then, if her brother doesn't turn up, we can start off. Tell you what," he added as if inspired, "we could telephone the hotel again, to find out if your brother's called there."

"There's one thing about Brian," Halloran said, "he thinks of everything."

They all chuckled.

Even the tall man who had followed them, and was listening from a spot between two mammoth cars, smiled so broadly that it looked as if he would like to laugh aloud. He waited until they were half-way towards the airport buildings, and then followed again. He watched them go in. He did not catch up with them but, five minutes later, he was within earshot when Brian Conway came out of a telephone booth and looked thoughtfully at Valerie. Mike Halloran, who proved to be rather a short man and not particularly broad, stood by the girl. His wide-brimmed hat denied most passers-by a view of the uniqueness of his face.

"I talked to the floor clerk this time," Brian Conway said, "and she tells me that your brother left the hotel at half-past eight. That should have given him plenty of time - more than plenty."

Now Valerie Hall looked really alarmed.

"Say, Miss Hall," said Halloran, as if seized by a great idea, "I sure hope that brother of yours hasn't run into any trouble."

2

COINCIDENCE

To Valerie Hall the journey from Idlewild Airport to the heart of Manhattan began at a furious speed, threatened to become a nightmare and at last, in spite of her anxiety for her brother, took her on the brink of wonderland again. The first mile or so seemed to be along wide, winding roads which led to nowhere at all, but in the distance there were the headlights of many cars, and soon they joined a mass of vehicles, all heading the same way, and all going at a speed which seemed suicidal. It was as if every driver put his foot down and then locked the controls, so that the car could not swerve either right or left. Every now and again all the cars nearby seemed to slow down at the same moment; then all began to surge forward at precisely the same time.

Next they drove along a wide road, with service roads on either side, and shops which were so brightly lit that it might have been daylight itself. Many shops were open, which surprised Valerie. The streets were thick with people, too.

They came to the long, dark approaches to a bridge.

"Here's Queensborough Bridge," Conway told Valerie Hall, and they swept up a wide roadway towards the main span of the bridge, and suddenly came upon the wonderland. Great buildings, rising to vast heights, all shimmered with countless lights; not one but a hundred of these were lit up, as if by magic. The wheels hummed noisily over the bridge, and then gradually the fairyland faded. They came to one sharp corner, then a second - and were soon in a flow of traffic heading west.

"Now we're really here," Conway said, with satisfaction. "This is 52nd Street. We'll be at the Arden-Astoria any moment now, and there might be a message for you." ...

"Thank you," said Valerie.

The fascination was beginning to fade, and anxiety took its place. Brian Conway seemed to understand all this, and his hand closed over hers. They were sitting in the front of the car, with Halloran at the wheel, and Valerie in the middle. Halloran was a single-purpose driver, and except to curse mildly at one or two other motorists, hadn't opened his mouth all the way. Now, in the brightness of the New York street, he proved to know his way around almost as well as a taxi-driver, and soon he delivered them to Park Avenue and slid to a standstill outside the unimpressive entrance of the Arden-Astoria.

"You take good care of Miss Hall," he said. "I'll park the car and be right back." If he had lived with grizzlies during each of the past five years he could not have had a gruffer voice.

"Right," said Conway. "Do that."

He handed Valerie out.

As they stepped into the hotel, a red-and-yellow taxi drew up behind, taking the place of Mike Halloran's sky-blue Ford, which slid silently away. Out of the taxi there stepped the tall, dark man who had been so interested in the girl while at the airport, and who had flown in the same stratocruiser. He watched Mike's car out of sight, and then went into the hotel. Conway and the girl were at the reception desk, talking earnestly. A bell-boy approached the dark-haired man, and asked:

'Can I help you, sir?"

"Later, thanks," the man said.

"Yes, sir."

There were bright lights in show-cases, models, jewels,

perfumes and cosmetics in priceless containers. There were thick carpets and luxuriously comfortable chairs. Smartly uniformed bell-boys were dotted about, and lads, a little taller, were at the elevators. Oddly, few other people were about, and an elderly man with a bald patch in his white hair, and a little woman with obviously aching feet, looked out of place and pathetic.

Valerie said: "But what shall we do? What can have happened to him?" She didn't actually utter the next sentence, but obviously it was at her lips: "He must have met with an accident."

She looked sweet, pretty, desirable and alarmed.

"You could call..." began a reception clerk who looked as if his clothes should be on a dummy in one of the showcases.

Conway did not let him finish.

"Don't you worry, Valerie; don't worry at all. Let me take you to your room, and then I'll get busy finding out what there is to find. I wouldn't be surprised to learn that he had a puncture or some trouble with his car - why, it would even be possible that we passed him on the road. Just don't worry. Mike and I will sort things out for you."

"You're so good, but..."

"Just forget it, and leave the worrying to us," urged Brian Conway. He gripped Valerie's arm tightly, then looked at the clerk. "We'll go right up to Miss Hall's suite," he declared.

"Yes, sir." The clerk raised a hand for a bell-boy, and the wheels of the hotel were set in motion. Bell-boys to elevator, elevator to Floor Clerk, Floor Clerk to chambermaid and porter who were waiting in the room with Valerie's luggage. Conway dispensed tips, and they were left alone in a huge room; a beautiful one, which looked as if it should be in a castle or some stately home - there was too much munificence for a hotel. A thick cream-coloured carpet, exquisite furniture, exquisite lampshades, including a small chandelier of Waterford glass or a very fine imitation. There was a sitting-room which would hold fifty people, when standing, and beyond was a bedroom with one canopied bed and pale-blue satin drapes. Off this, a queenly bathroom.

Conway took a swift look round.

"Everything seems fine," he said. "Now, Valerie, you only have to tell me if there's anything else you want."

"All I want is news about Wilf," said Valerie Hall.

"Sure; but don't you worry, Mike will be back by now and we'll get busy," Conway promised her. "In my experience the worst thing you expect never happens - why, when I put every penny I had into Mike Halloran's hands, five years ago, I seemed as if I was parting with my heritage. It was every penny I had. And Mike walked off with it. You know Mike; ask yourself if you would have liked the idea. I hardly knew the guy in those days, but he sold me on this prospecting, told me he had staked a claim to some hundreds of square miles right in the north of Quebec, country so wild that man hadn't set foot in it before. But he knew there was uranium there, and oil too. All he needed was staking, and I told myself I could judge men. Was I right!" Conway laughed again, on that excited, triumphant note. "But it was nearly five years before I knew I was. Then Mike arrived back in New York and he cabled me the good news. Came over here a month ago, then went back to settle my affairs in England for a little while, and now I'm back with Mike, ready to cash in. And what might have happened? He might have been a confidence trickster, ready to walk off, but" Conway broke off.

Somehow he had managed to hold Valerie's interest, and for a few minutes the nagging anxiety about her brother had faded. She watched the strong, handsome face, while Conway slid a hand into his coat pocket, and then brought it out.

He held a small stone about the size of a pigeon's egg, but rough instead of smooth.

"That's what he gave me as security," he said. "That's my talisman for the rest of my life. A little piece of rock, worth how much? Worth nothing - until you run the Geiger counter over it. Then you get the rattle, then you know there's radio-active material in that piece of rock, and it's called uranium! And there's another word for uranium, Valerie - money. Fortune! Why, if you knew"

He broke off again, and this time his expression was ludicrous. He slipped the rock away, took both her hands, and gave an apologetic little laugh.

"What's the matter with me, Valerie? I'm really sorry; I know how worried you are; I was forgetting. But this piece of rock shows you how worried you can get without any need. I wouldn't mind betting that your brother will turn up before long, and you'll be as happy as you've ever been. You start unpacking, and I'll go and make some inquiries."

"All right," Valerie said. "How long will you be?"

"I won't be a minute longer than I can help," Conway promised. "Not a second, take it from me."

He squeezed her hands, and went out.

After he had gone, she watched the door for several seconds and then, still worriedly and very thoughtfully, she went across to a window and looked through the net curtains. Slowly she pulled one aside. Park Avenue wasn't brilliantly illuminated, like some of the other streets, but there was light enough. Cars flashed by. Some people strolled. Not far away there were lights of a hundred colours, and they spread their glow high into the sky.

Valerie turned away from the window.

It wasn't easy to get on with the unpacking, or to take her mind off her fears for her brother, or her doubts - inescapable doubts - about Conway and Halloran, who were so obviously confidence tricksters that it was inconceivable that they believed they had fooled her.

She opened a case, took out a few things, put them in a drawer - and then went to the window again, as if she could hope to see her brother from there. She was at the window for nearly three minutes, and still looking out when the telephone bell rang.

She swung round, and her eyes lit up.

"It'll be Wilf!" She flew across the room to the bed and snatched up the telephone from the bedside table. "Hallo!" she cried. "Wilf, darling!"

"Just a minute, please; I have a call for you," the operator said, and kept her waiting. She dropped on to the foam-rubber comfort of the bed, and sank into it. She leaned back and drew her legs up, curled there with her head on the pillow, a sight to warm the heart and excite the hopes of any man. The belief that the caller was her brother might be illogical, but for these few seconds it drove fear away.

Then:

"Is that Miss Valerie Hall?" The voice was rather hoarse, and unmistakably American; not Wilf's. Disappointment made Valerie sit up, slowly; worriedly.

"Yes," she said.

"Listen, Miss Hall," the man said quickly; "your brother's in bad trouble, and you've got to help him quick. Can I come and see you right now?"

She didn't speak; fear seemed to paralyse her.

"May I come and see you right now?" the man demanded, and his voice rose. "I think I can help, but there isn't any time to lose."

"Plea - please come at once," Valerie said, and then with a rush: "Where is my brother, what . . ."

She didn't finish, for the man rang off.

Valerie put the receiver down slowly, and moved away from the bed, but this time she did not go near the window. She had no idea how long the caller would be; 'at once' might mean almost any time within the next half-hour. Or longer? She just didn't know; but she was much more frightened now.

What had he meant by 'trouble'? By big trouble.

It seemed part of a pattern. Wilf missing, Conway and Halloran out to impress her and win her confidence, and now this. She found herself looking at the door; moving towards it; and when she heard a sound outside, she actually wrenched it open to see who was there.

It was a stranger, but she didn't think it was the man who had telephoned. She had seen this man before, and anyhow there was no sense of urgency about him. He was tall and startlingly good-looking. He had an air. He was smiling as he strolled towards the door from the corner of the passage, and he seemed to be too far away to have made the sound which she had heard. His face was tanned, his grey eyes were very bright and somehow very gay.

She stood staring.

He paused. "Hallo," he said; "can I help you?"

Valerie said: "No!" much more explosively than she had meant to, and drew back sharply. She didn't see what happened to his smile, did not even have time to see whether he went past or not. She closed the door, and immediately wondered why she had shouted, why he had frightened her; it was hard to imagine any sight more reassuring than the well-dressed, handsome Englishman with the Mayfair look and - that air. It was as if he found her and the whole wide world amusing.

It was an odd coincidence that he was in this passage at the same hotel, but she supposed that several people off the aircraft had come to the Arden-Astoria; it wasn't really remarkable.

Forget him.

Where was Wilf? What was his danger? When would the man who had telephoned come?

The thought was hardly in her mind before the apartment door-bell rang. This time, she moved more slowly, staring at it; and her hand went to her breast, as if to quieten her pounding heart. After a moment's pause - far too short a time - the bell rang again; and as she moved more quickly it rang for a third time.

"Oh, don't be in such a hurry!" she cried aloud, but now she moved swiftly, reached the door and opened it.

Before she could get out of the way, it was thrust hard against her.

"What . . ." she began, and then fear rose starkly. All the things she had heard about the crime in New York flashed into her mind, she uttered a sharp scream, then tried to push the door to.

She could not.

A man was leaning against the door - a heavy man, who prevented her from closing it. The odd thing was that he made no sound.

3

HELP

IN those few seconds after she had screamed, and before she saw more than the man's hand, Valerie Hall was less terrified. She was badly scared, but much more herself. The seconds passed very quickly; just a flash of time. Then, still supporting the door, she edged to one side so that she could see the man more clearly. He was leaning heavily against it. His head was lowered, and she saw dark, curly hair. He wore a light grey suit. His left arm was stretched out, and he clutched the edge of the door. As she stared, she saw his fingers gradually relax, until he lost his grip and slumped down further.

She said in a low-pitched voice: "Oh."

She knew now that the man was hurt, for he had collapsed completely. She heard his heavy breathing - laboured and tense. If she let the door go, he would fall and the door would bang back against the wall.

She needed help.

She could hardly think, beyond that.

This might be the man who had telephoned her - who else was it likely to be?

She edged towards him, gradually, wondering how she could save him from falling and then bring him in. She did not hear the faint sounds of someone approaching. Odd thoughts flashed through her mind; that this man had been taken ill, had rung for help, had tried desperately to make her open the door before collapsing.

If she pushed the door back, now, he would fall against her and she could hold him up, drag him into the room and then telephone for....

She fought back a scream.

There was blood on the man's back - blood at his neck, collar, coat - red, spreading blood.

He fell heavily against her, and the shock of what she had seen robbed her of strength. She staggered back beneath his weight. Somehow, she managed to save them both from falling, but it was only by thrusting her arms round him; and her hands met at the back of his waist and there was the warmth of blood on her fingers.

This time, she didn't scream.

Then, the dark-haired Englishman appeared again.

He came in and closed the door before she could speak, and then without showing the slightest surprise or alarm, he put his hand beneath the wounded man's arms, and eased him back from her, while keeping him at arm's length. As he did so, there was a sound in the throat of the wounded man, a kind of rattle. Valerie had never heard anything like it before, and had not the slightest idea what it was. She felt a great surge of relief; for here was help, the wounded man was no longer in her arms, the tall Englishman still held him up. She saw that he was wearing a plastic raincoat, but didn't give that a thought then; a moment later she was shaken out of herself, for he lifted the big, heavy stranger right off the ground; then he said quietly:

"Get my key out of my right jacket pocket, will you? It's Suite 552, next door. Go along and open the door, leave it ajar, and go and wash your hands in my bathroom."

Valerie stared blankly.

"But- ..."

"If you don't do it quickly," the man said, "you'll spend your first few days in New York in and out of police stations. I should hurry if I were you."

He smiled.

As Valerie moved, slipped her hand into the Englishman's pocket for his key, and then hurried out of the room, she kept seeing that smile. It hadn't been simply one of amusement, and it hadn't seemed out of place. Instead, it had given her a reassurance, taking away some of the bewilderment and the fear. It wasn't until she was handling the key and opening the door of Suite 552 that she remembered that her hands were bloody; and sticky. She shivered. The door opened, and she went inside, careful not to touch anything with those sticky hands. She had never realised how bright was human blood. She began to shiver again as she walked across the first room towards the bathroom, and stepped inside. She ran water into the hand-basin - and as she dipped her hands in, it became crimson. She emptied it; the next lot of water was only pink, but that didn't reassure her. She couldn't stop trembling; even when she had dried her hands, she was quivering from head to foot.

She heard sounds.

She went out of the bathroom, and saw a startling thing: the tall Englishman, just inside the room, with the heavy man leaning against the door, much as he had against hers, but inside this room, not outside. The Englishman moved swiftly and then lifted the unconscious man again.

He drew him to the bathroom, and stretched him out on the tiled floor.

Something in the limpness of the unknown's body, the way his hands and arms flopped, warned Valerie of the truth, but it didn't sink in. She was obsessed by her own fears and, now, by greater fears for her brother. Yet when she tried to speak she couldn't form words, she was trembling so much with nervous reaction. She was angry with herself, because she didn't usually give way like this, but she couldn't help herself.

The tall man smiled again.

That calmed her a little.

Then he spoke very quietly.

"If you'll do exactly what I tell you, we'll see this through. Go back to your own apartment and take that suit off - there may be spots of blood on it. Just hang it in th+e wardrobe, making sure it doesn't touch any other clothes. Put on another suit that looks like it, if you can - if not, change completely. If there's any blood on the inside of the room door, wipe it off - and if there's any on the carpet, telephone me at once. Just tell me that something's spilled; don't talk of blood. Suite 552, remember. And incidentally" - he smiled again, and actually reassured her - "my name is Rollison."

His instructions were clear enough; and something in his manner warned Valerie that she must obey.

What else could she do?

"All - all right," she said, and went out.

She wondered what he would do with the man; whether he would send for a doctor, how badly the man was hurt, and - who had attacked him. Who, and how? She had heard nothing but the ringing - three short, sharp rings - and had lost her nerve.

Never mind that.

Had it been the wounded man who had telephoned to tell her that Wilf was in such trouble?

She pushed the door of her own suite open, and didn't see any red spots on the cream-coloured paint. She went inside, closed the door, and saw several small spots on the carpet; they were more brown than red, and she didn't think anyone was likely to notice them, but she had to telephone the man - what was his name?

Rollison, that was it; Rollison.

She had so much to do. Too much.

Being suddenly busy made it easier not to lose her self-control. She had to keep calm. That's what Wilf would say, that was what her father would have said before he died. In a crisis keep calm. More people lost their heads through losing their self-control in a crisis. Keep calm. The precise instructions of the man named Rollison made that easier to achieve, too. She went into the bedroom, and looked at herself in the mirror of the huge dressing-table. There were spots of blood on the small black-and-white check, as well as several on her blouse; and, like those on the carpet, they had lost their brightness and were more brown than red. She hurried to the wardrobe, and exclaimed with annoyance because she found it empty; of course she hadn't unpacked. What was happening to her? Keep calm.

She took off her jacket, skirt and blouse. Her white silk slip clung to her figure, but she didn't give her reflection a glance. She had no other two-piece like the one she had taken off, but there was a dress of the same material, and she put that on. Then she hung up the suit, with the blouse beneath it. When that was done, she went to the telephone, and asked for Suite 552.

Rollison answered almost at once.

"This - this is Valerie Hall," she said. "I thought - I thought I ought to tell you, a little dropped."

"Only a little?" he asked.

"Yes, you'd hardly notice it."

"Then leave it," the man Rollison said. His voice, quiet and pleasant, was almost as reassuring as her smile. "How long will your new friends be, do you know?"

"Brian Conway?" She hesitated. "No, I don't. He-he was going to try to find out where my brother was, but . . ."

"Hold it a moment," Rollison interrupted, and she found herself obeying, automatically. "I haven't time to wait now; just tell me how near I am to it. Your brother wasn't at the airport to meet you, and Conway's gone to look for him. You had a telephone message from a stranger saying that your brother was in trouble, and would you see the stranger right away? You said yes, and when he came he was leaning against the door." Rollison paused, and then asked quietly: "Is that right?"

She exclaimed: "It - it's uncanny!"

There was a hint of laughter in Rollison's voice.

"Some people would find another word for it," he said. "Now, be patient a little longer. When Conway and his friend come back, don't tell them what's happened. Appear as worried as you like about your brother, but say nothing about the visitor. If they ask you if anyone called, say no. And if they want you to leave the apartment, don't. Offer any excuse you like, but don't leave the apartment with them or with anyone else until I've told you that it's all right to go."

Valerie cried: "But why?"

"Your brother seems to be lost, and we don't want to lose you too," Rollison said dryly. "Don't worry too much, don't talk too much - I'll see you before very long."

She couldn't let it go at that.

"But who are you, why are you doing this, how did you know"

"If I were you," Rollison interrupted, in that quiet and confident voice, "I should take things very easily - and have a drink to calm your nerves. I know it's difficult, but if you want to help Wilf, do just as I say."

"But . . ." Valerie began again, gaspingly.

He rang off.

She put the receiver down slowly, but didn't get up from the side of the bed. The room seemed so very quiet, now. She looked through the open door towards the passage door, and could not see the spots on the carpet. She looked down at her hands; they seemed quite clear of blood. So did her stockings. She didn't ring for service, but went to her travelling case, took a small gold flask and unscrewed the cap and sipped a little brandy. After a few minutes, she sipped a little more. As she put the flask away, she realised how badly frightened she was, and as she stood up from an easy-chair, she understood how much worse she would have felt if she had been on her own; if it had not been for the man next door. But who was he? Confidence tricksters sometimes worked in groups.

She remembered his name: Rollison.

She thought that she had heard the name before, and now she began to tell herself that his face was familiar. It wasn't only that she had seen him at London airport; her recollection was of a meeting a long time before that. Or had she seen his photograph? She couldn't think beyond that point, but made herself think of Wilf, and what might have happened to him, and she shivered again.

What about Conway?

Should she do what Rollison said, and not tell Conway of the visit, the wounded man, the blood ...

She felt rather better, now; the brandy was helping. She moved to the open suitcase on the luggage-stand, and began to unpack, doing everything very slowly and with great precision. She was glad that Wilf hadn't arranged for her to have a maid here; a maid would have complicated the situation hopelessly, and it was bad enough now. Whenever she stopped working, it was as if a wave of terror began to sweep over her; only by keeping busy could she hold it at bay.

Could she hide the truth from Conway?

Perhaps when he came back he would say that he had news of Wilf. If he had, then Rollison could talk as much as he liked, she would do whatever Conway wanted. There was no way of being sure that he was a rogue.

Valerie heard a sound at the door.

The wave of fear threatened again, and she spun round, with her hands raised. The sound might have been a footfall; she just wasn't sure. She felt rigid, and yet began to tremble. The sound wasn't repeated and an age seemed to pass before she began to relax; as soon as she did, the bell rang.

She gasped: "No!"

Her nerves had never been so bad; perhaps because she was tired - she'd hardly slept the previous night. Whatever the cause, she was in a hopeless mood.

She closed her eyes, and swayed; and then gradually fought to regain control of herself. It was the sound of the ringing bell and the memory of what it had heralded before that had affected her, but - keep calm. Her father had made his millions by following that axiom among many others.

She drew herself up, felt better, and went quickly to the door. As she went, she hoped that the caller would not ring again; yet the interval seemed unending, she couldn't get to the door quickly enough. If it rang.

It rang.

She jumped; and then clenched her teeth. For a moment she hesitated - and then she heard Brian Conway's voice.

"Valerie, are you there? Valerie?"

He rang again, but her fears were gone; she need not dread opening the door to find a man leaning against it, with blood on his neck and his back. At last, she opened the door and Conway stood looking at her; Halloran was just behind, his craggy, ill-shaven face looking like the valley of a thousand hills.

Everything was all right.

Well, Brian Conway was all right....

His expression had changed. He wasn't really the same; not hurt, not scared, not dishevelled but - grimmer; much more grim. As if he brought bad news. With that thought, all the dread Valerie had felt returned, with all her fears for Wilf. She drew back into the room, hands clenched, almost at screaming point as Conway followed her and Halloran came behind.

Halloran closed the door; it was as if he shut out hope.

4

ILL TIDINGS

Valerie said: "What's the matter?" in a whisper which she could hardly hear herself. When Conway drew closer to her, with that set, grim face, she made herself cry: "What's happened? What's the matter?"

"Now take it easy," Brian Conway ordered. He took her hands and held them tightly; almost possessively. "It isn't as bad as all that, Val; just take it easy."

"What has happened to Wilf?"

"Now listen, ma'am," said Halloran in that rock-hard voice; "nothing's happened to your brother, and if you're careful I guess nothing will. So, ma'am, don't take on so."

He closed his mouth; it was like closing a trap.

Conway slid an arm round Valerie's shoulders.

"Take it easy, Val," he said, "and everything will be all right. You needn't worry; Mike and I will see to that."

Make gave a portentous nod; had Valerie been less terrified and blind with fears, she would have seen how ridiculous Halloran was; like a small-part player stealing a Hollywood quickie. As it was, her common sense told her that these men were in some plot to cheat both her and Wilf.

Wilf!

"Wilf's fine, just fine," Conway told her, and gulped.

That, and the grimness of his expression, told Valerie that it wasn't true; whether he was responsible or not, he was bringing her bad news. She wrenched herself free, and cried:

"Will you tell me what's happened to Wilf?"

"Sure, Brian, tell her," Halloran said.

Conway moistened his lips.

"Now take it easy," he repeated, as if he was afraid that Valerie would throw herself at him, or fly into hysterics. "He's been - kidnapped, that's all."

"Sure," nodded Halloran. "Snatched."

For a few seconds, the word was just a word: snatched. Valerie had feared nearly every catastrophe: a road accident, murder, illness; and yet she hadn't even thought of Wilf being kidnapped. It was a word which had no personal meaning, an archaic kind of word, conjuring up visions of the Caribbean Sea, pirates and buccaneers; or, in these modern days, sensational stories in gaudy newspapers. It had never had any flesh-and-blood significance, no part of daily life. Yet, as she stared rather stupidly at Conway, she began to realise how it fitted in with her suspicions of him. And she should have suspected it - kidnapping, ransom - oh, it all fitted in. But all she could say, very weakly, was:

"What?"

"Snatched," repeated Halloran.

"You mean - kidnapped?" Now that it was beginning to make sense, it brought worse fear. She didn't know how to react; all she could think of was Wilf, in danger. If it meant paying out a fortune, she had to get him back.

"You mean Wilf's been kidnapped? Who..." She choked, hating herself for the folly of the words. "Why..."

"They want a hundred thousand dollars," Conway blurted out.

"And boy," said Halloran, "is that big money?"

Valerie backed to a chair, and sat down. Conway was too late to help her. She leaned back and closed her eyes for a moment, and when she opened them again both men were staring at her, as if anxiously. How well they acted, now!

Halloran put his right arm behind him, and produced it again, carrying a leather-covered flask.

"It's rye," he said. "What do you think, Brian?"

"Val, would you like a spot of whisky?"

"No," Valerie said. "No, thank you." She felt swimmy, but two words were rising out of the mists in her mind, like bubbles rising to the surface of a whirlpool. Keep calm. "No, I'll be all right," she said; "just leave me alone for a while."

"Brave little woman," Halloran opined, while he kept a completely straight face.

Valerie heard him, but didn't think about what he said. She was trying to get the simple facts clear in her mind, and the only one which really mattered was this news about Wilf. The incident of the telephone call and the injured man falling into her arms might never have happened.

Conway lit a cigarette.

Valerie spoke in a much steadier voice. "I suppose you two do know what you're saying. Wilf has been kidnapped?"

Oh, yes," said Conway.

"Sure," asserted Halloran.

"It was like this," said Conway, beginning to pace the room; now he looked much more harassed and worried than Valerie, and was rather over-playing his part again.

"When we got downstairs we asked the desk clerk to put us in touch with the nearest hospital, and then the hospitals on the way to Idlewild. Before he could do that a man came and told me he had a message from your brother. He—"

"How did he know you?" asked Valerie.

"This is just the way it happened," Conway explained earnestly. "We were followed from the airport, and the kidnappers saw you with us. And they had another man, waiting right here, to see what we would do. He was the man downstairs, who spoke to me. Mike and I went outside with him; we didn't dream what kind of message it was. I mean, would you have guessed?"

Valerie shook her head.

"He simply told us that your brother had been kidnapped, and that he'd be released in return for a hundred thousand dollars," Conway continued. "And" He broke off, and gulped.

"Please go on," Valerie made herself say.

"He said that they hadn't much time," Conway went on; "they want to get out of New York tonight, and if you don't pay up quickly, then"

He stopped, as if he simply couldn't bring himself to finish.

"Murdering lot of hoodlums," Halloran said.

"Murdering." Valerie gasped.

"Now take it easy," Conway rebuked.

"But I haven't got a hundred thousand dollars! It would take me days to get it," Valerie cried. "I've only a credit for twenty thousand. They can't do it, they can't . . .;'

"Now listen to me, ma'am," said Halloran. He put his hand into the inside pocket of his jacket, and when he drew it out he held a wallet which looked as thick and solid as the whisky-flask. "We can rustle up some dollars to help, I guess. I've close on five thousand right here, and Brian - how many you got, Brian?"

"Three thousand," Brian answered, as if miserably.

"That makes eight," declared Halloran, after a long and pregnant pause. He paused again. "Sure, that's right. That makes eight. Eight from one hundred is how many? Eight-two." He paused again. "Sure, that's eight, eighty - no, ninety-two. Wait a minute." He screwed up one eye and began to count on his fingers.

"Mr. Conway," Valerie said, and caught her breath. "What - what are we going to do? They can't - they can't mean" She broke off again. She felt so sure that these two men were involved in the plot, and Halloran looked as if he could kill without compunction.

"If you ask me," said Brian Conway solemnly, "they mean just what they said. There's no way of being sure; you could take a chance that they'll just beat your brother up, but - well, why should they let him go? This man told me that he knows how rich you are - you and Wilf. He knows that you've inherited the Hall millions on this side, and you are very rich in England, anyway. He said that you ought to think yourself lucky that he's only asking for a hundred thousand."

Conway stopped being the perfect mouthpiece.

"If it was tomorrow," Halloran said, "we could get the money, except for one thing. Tomorrow's Sunday."

"It's hell," breathed Brian. Valerie put her hands to her ears. The diamond stud earrings were worth a little more than a thousand pounds; nearly three thousand dollars. Her rings twice as much. The other jewellery in her travelling-case, much more. She looked from Conway to Halloran, doing mental arithmetic with feverish intentness. Then suddenly she said:

"They can have my jewels." She had nearly said: "You can." "I've fifty thousand dollars' worth with me. And if you'll lend me what you have, that will make sixty thousand altogether." She had to keep up the pretence of trusting them. "They must accept sixty thousand."

She caught her breath.

Conway said dubiously: "Perhaps they will."

"Could be," chimed in Halloran. "Sixty thousand ain't a hundred thousand, it's quite a pile less. Lemme see." He closed one eye again. "Sixty and ten thousand makes . . ."

"But I must be sure they'll release Wilf," Valerie said. She jumped up suddenly, and Conway was so close that he backed hastily away. "How can I make sure? Where is this man? What did he ask you to do next?"

"He said we're to check the money in a locker at Grand Central Station," Conway told her. "Then we're to go away, and hand the key to a man who'll be in the concourse. He'll go and open the locker, and if the money's there"

Valerie broke in: "What on earth are you talking about? Locker, concourse, check - what is all this?" Her eyes were glittering, and she walked to and fro in feverish haste which wasn't pretended. "And who on earth thinks I'm going to be such a fool as to hand over a hundred thousand."

"Sixty," interpolated Halloran.

"A hundred, two hundred, sixty, seventy, what difference does it make?" cried Valerie. "Who on earth thinks I'm going to be fool enough to hand over any money or my jewels or anything at all unless I'm sure they'll release Wilf? What's to stop them from taking the money and then asking for more tomorrow or next week? I'm not that simple!"

But, if the worst came to the worst, she would be; for Wilf.

Conway looked more dejected even than before.

"I've only told you what he said," he claimed.

"Where is this man?" demanded Valerie.

"He's outside, at the corner of Park and Fiftieth, and he said he'd wait there an hour."

"An hour?"

"Yes."

"Listen," said Valerie, moving towards Conway quickly and taking his arm. "Why shouldn't we call the police? They could follow this man, and"

"No, ma'am," broke in Halloran, in fierce alarm, "don't you go telling the police! No, ma'am. Do you know what he threatened to do if you was to tell the police? Why, he threatened to kill your brother, and find a way to kill you. Yes, ma'am. And the way that guy talked, he meant just what he said. You keep yourself right away from the police."

"If he thinks I'm afraid - -"

"Listen, Val," Conway interrupted, in a persuasive way; "we've got to look facts in the face. A lot of these New York crooks are desperate men. You don't need telling that. And" He broke off for a moment, gave the gulp that seemed so natural, and went on: "He said that one of the men behind the snatch - er - the kidnapping, was Dutch Himmy. You've never heard of Dutch Himmy, but he's one of the most brutal guys over here. If he says he'll kill, you can take it from me he'll kill."

"How many's he killed?" Halloran asked, ferociously. "Six?"

"Four or five," said Conway, flatly. "Val, it's a dreadful situation, but you've got to face up to it. These men mean business. Either you do what they say or you risk your brother's life. If you go to the police - well, I just won't let you," he declared bluntly; "it would be suicide." He took her arm.

"Curtains," chimed in Halloran.

Valerie freed herself, and hesitated.

Any lingering doubt had gone; these two men were in the plot, were out to squeeze every penny they could from her, and to frighten her into submission. And - she had to save Wilf.

When she spoke again it was more quietly. Her eyes no longer glittered, all sign of hysteria had gone, and she had a quiet vehemence which told how stubborn she could be. She felt better, too; much more herself.

"I don't know what you two think," she said, "but think that if these men have kidnapped Wilf so as to get a hundred thousand dollars, they want the money badly. They'll be quite as frightened of the police as we are. If they see even half a chance of getting part of the money, I think they'll jump at it. And only fools would expect anyone to hand over money like that without some kind of guarantee. I don't care who they are, Dutch Himmy or-German George or Russian Rudolph, they won't just go away and kill Wilf and throw away any chance they ever had of getting the money." She raised and shook a clenched fist. "I'll go and talk to this man! Where"

"Val, listen!" Conway cried. "They might do any thing; they might kill you. You've got to leave us to do the talking. If"

"Brian," said Halloran, deeply, "you want to know something? I think the little lady's right. Yes, sir; she's got more sense in that pretty little finger of hers than we have in our two heads. Yes, sir. I think that you and me both must go and talk to this guy, and make some arrangement with him. Yes, sir-ree. We'll tell him that Miss Hall will find sixty thousand bucks, or the equivalent of it, but in return she wants some guarantee that her brother will be released. Fair enough, ma'am?"

"I doubt if he'll agree," Conway muttered.

"Then the little lady says that if he doesn't agree, he doesn't get the money. Is that so, ma'am?"

Valerie said: "Yes," dubiously. It was difficult to keep up the pretence, hard not to tell them she knew what part they were playing. Then her voice strengthened and she squared her shoulders. "Yes!" she cried. "Go and tell him that, and please, hurry!"

Conway turned round, brow deeply lined and mouth drooping. Halloran walked firmly across to the door, opened it, and then turned round and raised a hand.

"Don't you worry, ma'am; we'll fix it for you," he said. "Come on, Brian." He beckoned, and Brian Conway went out slowly, as if he was a long way from confident.

The door closed.

Valerie turned round and flew towards the bedroom, went rushing across to the wardrobe, opened it, pulled out a raincoat, and turned on her heel as if she hadn't a moment to spare. She was going after them; she couldn't stay here, she ... But she didn't go.

She stopped absolutely still, in shocked horror.

A man stood behind the bedroom door; and must have been there for a long time. It was Rollison, from next door. But he'd gone out and hadn't come in. ...

Valerie opened her mouth to speak, but words wouldn't come.

"I thought I asked you not to go out," Rollison said mildly, and he moved across and took the raincoat from her.

"B-b-b-but ..."

"Didn't you think I meant it?"

"B-b-b-but how did you get in?" Valerie gasped;

"I didn't see you; I ..." She broke off, and looked at the wall between this room and the one next door. It was a blank wall; there was no possible way from one suite to the next; this was like looking at a ghost. "How - how did"

"I came in through the window," Rollison told her calmly. "I had a feeling that it would be worth lending an ear to the chatter. Bright pair, aren't they? Provided they haven't hurt your brother, I could almost like them."

Valerie said: "What?" in a squeaky voice.

"I shouldn't think they've really fooled you though," said Rollison. "I know they think they've done a beautiful job, but Conway played a bit too much ham. Hal-Ioran's almost too fantastic to be false; he's really the better of the pair. But never mind that. The problem is to find out where they've hidden your brother, without letting them realise that you know that the man round the corner is a myth or an accomplice."

Rollison paused, as if he meant to give Valerie a chance to get her breath back.

At least she wasn't alone in what she thought, but - could this man be another of them, a third partner who was pretending to come to her rescue?

If only she could remember where she had seen him before.

"And you were really going out after them," he marvelled. "How far do you think you'd have got?"

Valerie didn't answer, but looked away from him, then stepped firmly past him to the window.

It was open a little.

She pulled it wider, looked out, and glanced along towards Suite 552. A window there was open, too, although no light shone out into the night.

She said in a small voice: "Did you really ..." and then broke off, looking dizzily downwards. There were thirty storeys between here and the pavement, to an awful, thudding death. Cars below looked like toys, people like pigmies.

"You couldn't have," she breathed, and turned to stare at him again. "But if you did, if I have to believe that, then I suppose I ought to believe that you can be trusted."

He was smiling at her. There was a hint of mockery in his eyes; but a gentle mockery. Suddenly, he had become more than life-size; a kind of superman. He moved, slid his arm round her shoulders and hugged her, then spoke in the most nonchalant way in the world.

"You just need to believe that Brian and his Mike are deep in this game, and that I'm on your side," he said. "It has all the hallmark of the classic confidence trick, and con-men don't usually go in for violence, either side of the Atlantic. I should say that this pair have teamed up with someone else - it could even be this Dutch Himmy they talk about." He chuckled. "Or German George or Russian Rudolph! Certainly they won't kill the goose they hope lays golden eggs, as certainly we have to be very careful, because they have killed once, but..."

Valerie echoed sharply: "They have killed someone?"

"Oh, yes," said Rollison, and the light faded from his eyes, which became very hard and grim. "The man next door is dead. Didn't you guess?"

She hadn't guessed.

Now, she realised that she should have; and suddenly her fears for her brother rose almost to screaming pitch.

5

BRIGHT LIGHTS

THE Honourable Richard Rollison, known by many by the apt if absurd soubriquet of the Toff, studied Valerie Hall closely. He felt no surprise at her behaviour, but much admiration for her as a person. She was the stuff of which heroines were made, as he had been warned. She was small, she was slender, she looked fragile; rather like something which ought to be protected, as Dresden china; but in her way she was as tough as women came, and she had that reputation among her friends and relatives, too.

And in his way, the Toff was also tough....

He watched the varying expressions on Valerie's face. He made allowance for the shocks she had already had, for her fears for her brother and the fact that she now knew that murder had been done. In the thirty seconds which passed between the Toff's 'didn't you guess?' and her response, expressions chased one another across her face - shock, fear, dread, hopelessness, resolve, hope reborn, anger and, finally, determination.

It was quite a sight.

By the time the show was over, the Toff was smiling very broadly.

"What do you want me to do?" she asked, in a subdued voice. There was a pause; then she went on, more quickly: "I think you'd better tell me why I should trust you, and not the others. I don't know you, either."

Now he had proof that she could keep her head.

There was no desperate hurry to leave. Rollison was sure that the two men would not come back very quickly; they would allow some time to pass, so that when they returned, whatever message they gave Valerie would have the ring of truth; they would probably regale her with a story of how they had argued and pleaded with the man round the corner. So, Rollison took a letter from his pocket and handed it to the girl. She took it with her white, nicely-shaped hands. The envelope was addressed to the Honourable Richard Rollison, and after seeing that she glanced at him sharply, but didn't speak.

She opened the letter and glanced at the signature, which was Wilfred K. Hall.

"It's from Wilf!" she cried. "Do you know him? Do…" But she didn't finish what she was saying, just read the letter swiftly. Like that, with her eyes very bright and her lips parted, she looked quite at her best.

The letter read:

"The job's really very simple. I would like you to follow my sister, Valerie Hall, when she leaves London for New York, travelling on the same plane and staying at the Arden-Astoria to make sure that she's all right. Of course, I may be crazy, there may not be any need for anxiety, but I have an uncomfortable feeling that either Valerie or I might run into trouble. I won't go into details now. At best, it'll be a flip across the big pond and a few days wallowing in luxury at the A-A. At worst, it will mean trouble, but I don't need to tell the Toff anything about that!

"I'll arrange everything else with your man Jolly, of course. Thanks for easing my mind.

Yours,"

Valerie looked up again, with a different expression in her eyes; confidence. She studied Rollison's face very closely, then glanced at her watch, and said quietly:

"We'd better do something, hadn't we? They're bound to come back soon. I'm not sure you were right to stop me from going out; I was only going to follow them, and..."

"Not by yourself in New York," Rollison protested; "too many wolves are interested. Conway and Halloran will be back soon, and they'll say that this mystery man has agreed to the terms. They'll want to take your diamonds and everything else of value to him - and if you let them, that could easily be the last you'd hear of them. Wilf might possibly be released, but it's more likely that the gang will hold him and come back for more money when you've had time to lay your hands on some. If they're going to play it that way, then Halloran and Conway will stay around - one will offer to sleep in the sitting-room, as your gallant protector! But we needn't go into every detail, need we?"

"I want to know what to do" Valerie insisted.

Rollison grinned at her.

"One day some man's going to be very glad he met you," he said. "All right, woman of action. When they come back, you'll refuse to let Conway and Halloran act as intermediaries. You'll insist on going along and seeing this man they talk about yourself, and you'll also insist on getting some guarantee that Wilf won't be hurt."

"Supposing they won't give me one?"

"Let's cross the streams when we get to them," said Rollison, easily. "Your job's to make them think that you still look on Brian and Mike as heaven-sent friends."

Valerie grimaced.

"Just glance along the passage and make sure it's empty, will you?" Rollison asked. "I'd rather go back to my suite without risking the long drop."

"All right," agreed Valerie, but instead of turning round at once, she contemplated him thoughtfully. Then: "What are you going to do?"

"I want ten minutes to get ready, and then I'll follow you. You may not recognise me, but I promise that I won't be far away."

"I suppose you are the Toff," said Valerie, with a dubious frown; and before he could make any reply, went on sharply: "Oh, of course you are! Mr. Rollison, do you really think that Wilf's in danger?"

That needed an honest answer, not just comfort for comfort's sake.

"He could be," Rollison said, "but I don't think it's likely. If we play our hand well . . ."

"I won't let you down," she broke in fiercely.

"Fine," said Rollison. "Don't leave until I telephone you. I'll call, and then apologise for getting the wrong number. Any time after that you can leave."

Valerie nodded, and Rollison watched as she went to the door, peered along the passage, and then beckoned. She gave him a smile that was nearly radiant as he went out; then she closed the door firmly.

Rollison was busy for ten furious minutes.

First, he went to a linen-closet he had already spotted, took out some sheets and blankets, and carried them to his own suite. There was the dead man, youthful and with a strangely pleasant face, on the bathroom floor. Rollison ran through his pockets, and discovered that his name was Mark Quentin, with an address on Long Island.

Rollison made a mental note of this, then spread sheets and blankets on the floor, and his plastic raincoat, the blood-stained side up, on top of these. He lifted the dead man, put him on the raincoat, and wrapped him up, all his movements swift and yet gentle. He fastened the bundle with pins, then carried it to the wardrobe, put it inside, locked the door and pocketed the key.

Swiftly he took off the Savile Row suit, and put on another which was laid out on the bed. This was a subdued royal blue in colour* and beside it was a sky-blue necktie, adorned with hand-paintings of high mountains and a sunset of rich, red gold. Next to this was a ten-gallon hat, the same colour as the sunset. He seemed to slide into his clothes, and into a pair of suede shoes which matched the hat. Then he glanced at himself in a tall mirror.

He grinned, the shadow of tragedy lifting.

"You're quite something," he said; "nothing more glorious ever came out of Las Vegas." He took a cigar from a leather case and put it to the corner of his lips, and then saluted himself. "Hi, stranger," he said, and turned away.

He went out.

A coloured girl in a blue smock was pushing a big linen-basket towards double doors marked 'staircase'; these were just beyond the linen-closet. He looked at the big basket thoughtfully; it was large enough to take Mark Quentin's body.

But not now.

As he turned the corner, Rollison saw Brian Conway and Mike Halloran stepping out of the elevator. He wasn't surprised that they were too preoccupied to do more than glance at him; he doubted if they even noticed that he was there. The Floor Clerk did, and looked at him with an admiration not far removed from veneration.

"Hi, ma'am," he drawled, and no one from Texas could have sounded at once more unreal and yet more natural; "just been along to see my old pal."

"Is that so?" asked the Floor Clerk, faintly.

"Sure is, ma'am, sure is." Rollison pressed a Down button, and an elevator car slid to a stop, light showing through the little window. "Now I'm going out to have myself quite a time, quite a time, ma'am." He winked. "You bet." He winked again, and then the elevator gates opened and he doffed his great hat as he stepped in. Inside were a man and a woman; neither of them could help staring at him, and he beamed back with great good will. At ground-floor level he stood aside for them to leave, and then strolled into the lobby, goggled at by everyone in sight. He was quite sure that none of them recognised him.

He looked a different man. The cut of the clothes changed

his whole figure, and the hat was at just the right angle, with curled brims on either side. He was already tanned a dark brown, and mascara cautiously used gave greater brightness to his grey eyes. He strolled towards Park Avenue and stepped outside. Not far along were several waiting taxis. He went up to the third, and the cabby actually leaned out, to open the door.

"Thank you, sir," said Rollison, with great gusto; "you're mighty kind."

The cabby's expression suggested that he could not really believe that such good fortune could come his way.

He was a round and ruddy-faced man with a skull-tight cap, the big peak of which was pushed over his right ear. Black hair curled from beneath the edges of the cap in a dark halo. Here was a picture by Michelangelo in the driver's seat of a New York cab, and it didn't look out of place.

Rollison got in, at leisure, and the cabby glanced round: "Where to?"

Almost under his nose was a fifty-dollar bill. He had to move his head back, to squint at it. He shook his head, and the curls quivered.

"You pay me after the ride, bud," he said.

"I'm not sure that I want a ride, pardner," Rollison told him in a subdued roar. "I may decide to walk. Take this as a retainer, suh, a handsome retainer. If I decide to walk, then you follow me and see if you can contrive to keep me in sight. Because I may want to follow another taxi or a car in a hurry, and if I'm in a hurry there won't be any time to waste in arguing. If I don't need you between now and one o'clock, you can go home to your bed. Okay, suh?"

The cabby was already folding the bill.

"Have it your own way," he conceded. "Any way you like."

Rollison sat back, smoking a cigarette and not a cigar. Nothing of consequence happened in the next ten minutes. During them, he pondered certain facts. Wilf Hall, whom he knew reasonably well, had sent a cable before he had sent that letter; the cable had been to find out whether Rollison was free to help him. It was characteristic of Wilf Hall to talk and write vaguely; it might mean that he had nothing specific to talk about, but was just as likely to mean that he preferred not to talk about it. His great anxiety had been for Valerie, who had been determined to visit him in America; and Wilf had meant to make sure she didn't come unprotected.

Unless, of course, Rollison failed her.

That possibility did not greatly worry Rollison.

He had not been to New York for a long time, but on his previous visits he had come to know Manhattan well. He had friends, too. He believed that he could judge exactly the moment to stop trying to handle the situation himself, and call on those friends for help. Had it not been for the man who had died in Valerie's arms he would have believed that it was just a simple confidence trick, but - con-men didn't kill; not that way, anyhow.

Why had the caller been killed?

Apparently, because he had come to give Valerie a message; but he hadn't uttered a word that mattered.

Now, finding Wilf Hall was as important as taking care of Valerie. The Halls were worth a dozen fortunes, and it -was well worth risking the loss of Valerie's jewels and money to get a line on Wilf; but it would be good to avoid even that loss.

Rollison finished the cigarette and tossed the end out of the taxi window - and as he did so, Brian Conway and Valerie appeared. They were close together, in a kind of huddle, and looked towards the taxis. Rollison said: "Move off slowly, pardner," and watched the couple. Conway shook his head, and instead of coming forward, led the way to the corner and the traffic lights. "Can you do a U turn here?" asked Rollison.

"For you, I'll turn a somersault," the driver declared. "Hold tight, bud." He shot the car forward and then swung round, and when he drew up on the other side of the road opposite the Arden-Astoria, Valerie and Conway, still in a huddle, were halfway across the avenue. Conway was holding the girl's arm, and talking.

"This is where I leave you," Rollison said, and opened the door. "Keep your eyes open and try to catch up with me, pardner, if these one-way streets allow you."

"How could I miss you?" asked the cabby, and his grin split his round face. "So long, bud!"

Rollison was chuckling.

At a corner of the next street, Conway and Valerie turned round. Rollison caught up with them, as they headed towards Madison Avenue, walking quickly. There were a lot of bright lights, and it was easy to look at Valerie and to realise that she was perfection in pocket-size.   Her legs....

Madison - Fifth - Broadway.

Two things happened as they reached Broadway.

First, the light became so bright that it hardly seemed true. Night had become a garish day. The pavements were thronged, and no one seemed to be in a hurry. Restaurants were nearly full, a few shops were open; in one, where a thousand hats seemed to perch on stands in the window, there were eight or nine customers. All was noisy with a thousand cars. In the direction of Times Square, it looked as if every light in New York had been massed at this one spot, and that one had to walk through and on lights of a hundred colours.

The Toff was staggered, in spite of his previous visits; but not so badly that he missed the second thing.

A young man whom he had not seen before was now following Valerie and the earnest Conway. This young man had been waiting opposite the hotel. Rollison had not yet seen his face, but had a good view of the curly, reddish hair, the slender shoulders, the almost hipless body. The young man's movements were cat-like, possessing a kind of natural stealth.

At Broadway, the couple turned towards Times Square, and the hipless young man followed them.

As Rollison followed in turn, a great garish yellow-and-red taxi slowed down alongside him, and the cabby gave him an enormous wink and a gargantuan whisper:

"You okay, bud?"

Rollison gave him the thumbs up sign, and walked on. Three times, when the others were held up at traffic lights, he turned to look behind him, but he saw no sign of Mike Halloran and nothing to suggest that he was being followed.

At 45th Street, Conway and Valerie turned into a restaurant across the front of which was written in naming red: HAM 'N EGGS. The hipless young man was then ten yards behind them; he didn't go in, but turned and went down the next street, where the restaurant boasted another window and a sign in flaming yellow.

Rollison reached the doorway.

Inside were bright lights, a spotless bar, red-topped stools, and tables for four, with high-backed seats. Cooks in starched white and waitresses in pale blue had eager, hopeful looks.

Conway had taken Valerie to one of the tables, and they were sitting down. A man was already there; Rollison could just see the top of his head.

So there was a third man.

Rollison went in and took a seat at a corner of the counter, so that he was sideways on to the trio, and very close by.

6
START OF A JOURNEY

From his point of vantage, Rollison could see the man whom Valerie had gone to see; he could also see the top of Brian Conway's head, and the tip of Valerie's little white hat. When he glanced at the window, he had a view of the hipless young man, who was just outside.

His chief interest was in the man who had been waiting in the restaurant for Conway and Valerie. He liked nothing about the face and the sharp, bright eyes.

Everything else seemed so cosy.

Hunger teased Rollison as a young man wearing a spotless white smock and a white chef's hat came up and asked: "What's yours?"

"Ham and eggs," said Rollison in the Colonel's voice.

"Eyes open or closed?"

Rollison clutched at memory, while the young cook regarded him without impatience or affection. Memory came to the rescue.

"Closed," Rollison said, firmly.

"Want coffee?"

"You bet."

The cook turned his back, and cracked eggs into a basin, slapped them into a small steel frying-pan, added bacon, and then started a great sizzling. A girl had ordered coffee and cheesecake for the trio in the stall. Whatever they said was very low-pitched, and Rollison heard nothing except whispers. He wished he could see Valerie's face, but he had to judge the show she was putting up from the face of the man opposite her. It was interesting, after all. Small, pale, rather narrow, with close-set bright eyes, a small, pointed nose.

He did not have the look of a big shot.

He kept looking about him, at the door, and at the hipless man, but he did not pay any attention to Rollison.

His biscuit-coloured jacket had wide shoulders; there was probably plenty of room for a gun in a shoulder-holster.

Every now and again he said: "Yeh," and sometimes he said "Naw." Occasionally, Valerie's voice sounded, almost angrily; anyone within range would know that they were quarrelling, but was given no inkling about the cause of the trouble.

Brian Conway contributed nothing at all to the conversation; he stayed dumb and looked miserable.

There was a sudden, triumphant sizzling sound in front of Rollison. Then the shimmering steel frying-pan, containing two eggs and some streaky bacon fried in the whites, was slapped in front of him. This appeared as if by magic. The eyes of the eggs were covered, blessedly, with a pale film of white. A crusty roll and a dab of butter were placed by this, and a huge cup of coffee. Rollison had not realised quite how hungry he was.

He did realise that it was now nearly half-past twelve, and unless things moved quickly he would not be able to use the taxi again.

He finished eating, and was about to order more coffee when Conway stood up, and all the trio made a move. The man with the close-set eyes wasn't as tall as Conway, and he proved to be painfully thin. He led the way, and Valerie, tight-lipped and obviously angry, came next. Conway looked ill-at-ease as he brought up the rear. They all went out into Broadway.

Rollison slipped a dollar-fifty on to the counter, stood up and went into the side street.

The hipless man was also on the move again.

Rollison now knew that this man had a pleasant face, if not particularly handsome or even full of character. He quickened his pace to intercept the others, and Rollison thought that he was going to call to Valerie.

He did, in a clear voice:

"Miss Hall, can you spare me a minute?"

He was only a few yards away from the trio, and there was no doubt that Valerie and the others heard him. Valerie actually looked round. The thin-faced man gripped her arm tightly, and Conway stood between her and the hipless wonder, who called again:

"Miss Hall, can you- ..."

Then, in front of Rollison's eyes, the fantastic happened. Swiftly, ruthlessly, brutally. Two men appeared, one from behind the hipless wonder, one from the other side of the road. Rollison was only three yards away, but powerless to do anything about it until the attack was well under way. The hipless man's call was cut short, and a fist smashed into his mouth. His legs were hooked from under him, and he fell heavily. A toe-cap cracked at the side of his head, another into his ribs. His body seemed to shake. Two couples, coming out of HAM 'N EGGS, drew back hastily, and one of the men said sharply: "None of our business!" Another man, on the far side of the road, shouted: "What's going on?" and started across, but several cars came along and the lights were green; he had to wait. Rollison could see Valerie and the other two at the corner; they hadn't been able to cross, and he had to get close to them.

If he drew too much attention to himself by attacking the two thugs....

He didn't need to.

With a final kick, which shifted the hapless hipless man along the ground, the pair turned and moved swiftly towards Broadway and the mass of people there. By then someone was shouting: "Police!" and police whistles were shrilling. Two cops, with guns in their hands, appeared on the opposite corner as the lights changed. They came rushing across. Valerie and her companions passed them going in the other direction, and Rollison put as much space as he could between him and the youth who had been beaten-up. His height enabled him to see over most of the heads, and he saw a taxi draw up, at Conway's raised hand. They bundled the girl into it.

"Bud!" Rollison groaned.

A taxi slid alongside him.

"In a hurry?" asked his cabby, with huge delight.

Rollison tumbled in. The door slammed, and the cab moved off quite as swiftly as the one in front.

"Follow that red cab," Rollison said breathlessly.

"Okay. I got sense. I do all right?"

"You're not a man, you're a miracle."

The cabby's grin was so delighted that it almost split the broad face in two.

"I'm not a miracle, I'm just a goddam Yank," he said, and laughed with delight. "You want to know something? Okay, I'll tell you. I saw you go into that joint and I kept driving round the block; it was easy. You okay?"

"I'm fine."

"You see the way they beat up that guy?"

"I saw it." Rollison was lighting another cigarette.

"It sure is bad," said the cabby, no longer even slightly flippant, "the things these guys will do. In broad daylight, too." He meant that; and it was almost daylight here, anyone could be forgiven for assuming that this was a city which knew no night. "Some of these guys, they want frying. But the cops was quick. You see that? The cops was quick."

"They really put a move on," agreed Rollison.

"That's right," said the driver. "They was putting a move on quick."

He fell silent. That was not because of any great difficulty, at this stage, in keeping the red taxi in sight. They had moved two blocks and were waiting at traffic lights. A minute later, they turned into 42nd Street, and headed towards the East River. In minutes, they were out of the brightly lit section. Many shop windows were in darkness. High buildings stretched up, some of them almost out of sight. They passed the corner entrance to the Grand Central Station, and then the Commodore Hotel. There, to Rollison's relief, they turned up Lexington Avenue; had they gone straight on it would have been difficult for the cabby to follow without the men in the cab in front knowing.

On Lexington, the traffic lights were with them, they had a long, sweeping drive without having to stop, and were in the middle of a group of some thirty or forty cars; there was no danger here. The red cab kept to the middle of the road at first, but gradually it pulled over towards the right, as if it were going to turn.

Rollison's driver pulled over, too.

The red cab swung right into one of the streets. Instead of following, the driver of Rollison's cab put his foot down, and the taxi seemed to leap forward. In that wild moment, Rollison wondered if he had been fooled, if his taxi-driver worked for Conway and Halloran, and had waited until now to show it.

"You've lost ..." he shouted desperately.

"Sit right back!" the cabby roared. He reached the next turning, which would carry one-way traffic to the left, instead of to the right, and swung into it the wrong way. A stationary car, waiting at the traffic lights, was so close that Rollison thought they were bound to crash. They missed by a fraction. No other cars were coming, and the cabby reached the next avenue, swung into it, cut across the path of two yellow cabs and forced them over, then swung into the next turning - the street into which Valerie's cab had been taken.

Tyres squealed.

The cabby slowed down.

"Okay?" he squeaked.

Red lights at the next intersection were holding up a solitary vehicle. As they drew nearer, it proved to be a red taxi; the red taxi.

"Okay," Rollison breathed.

The lights changed, and the two cars started off almost simultaneously. Rollison's cabby got his nose in front and kept that way for the next block, then allowed the other cab to overtake him. Had he been driving himself, Rollison would not have done this half as well. When the red cab slowed down again, outside a house in a street which led from Second Avenue to the East River, the three people in it could hardly suspect that the cab behind had followed.

As Rollison passed, he saw Valerie being helped out, and Conway already on the pavement, the other man crouching in the cab. None of them looked at him. He saw a number over the front door of the tall, narrow house: 48. He let his driver take him round the corner, and as they stopped he had another twenty-dollar bill in his hand.

The cabby squinted.

"Cheese, naw," he said; "you paid me."

"This is for waiting for the next hour," Rollison said, "say opposite number 38."

"Sure, that's okay, then," the cabby conceded. "It's not as if I need any sleep." He pocketed the twenty. "Bud," he said, "you wouldn't be walking into any trouble, would you? Not like that guy who was beaten up on 47th. Ain't none of my business, but you're a stranger around here, and some of these guys"

"Just a good girl friend of mine," said Rollison, "mixed up with the wrong boy friend."

The cabby said: "Well, if it's okay, okay. Take good care of yourself." He drove off, and Rollison turned away from the taxi and approached Number 48. He already knew that this was East 13th Street.

As he reached Number 48, two men leapt at him from the doorway. The light shining from it showed them to be the two who had attacked the hipless wonder.

7

THIRD FLOOR BACK

THE two men made one mistake as they fell upon Rollison; they came one at a time. Probably, the first was meant to floor the victim, the other to start the kicking and hacking process. It did not quite work out that way. The first man, hands raised as he plunged and feet ready to hook Rollison's legs from under him, felt his right arm grabbed. The world suddenly turned upside down. Rollison saw him curving a neat arc, about eight feet off the ground, but didn't wait to hear him fall; for the other man was not far away, and this other man had a knife.

Rollison shot out a leg.

The second assailant had no time to back away; at full pelt he ran into the foot which was stiff and straight, as if fastened to the end of an iron bar. The breath was driven out of his body in a long, anguished groan. The knife flickered and flashed, but he didn't let it go. Seeing him staggering back, Rollison glanced round to make sure that the first man was still on the ground and taking little notice, then went bodily into the attack. He was not simply annoyed, or just acting in self-defence. He was savagely angry, for he could see the hipless wonder in his mind's eye. Fist to stomach brought a gusty groan; fist to jaw brought a crack that sounded like bone breaking; another to the jaw tipped the man almost head over heels. This time he lost his grip on the knife and it went flying.

Then, two things happened.

A car or cab turned into the road, and the first man leapt. He also carried a knife. The faint light from the doorway showed a face which might have been a model for Epstein; as brutish as human faces come, with expression to match. As the car or cab came hurtling on, Rollison went like a bullet to meet this jungle throwback, and his left hand shot out, to grip the wrist of the knife-hand.

For a moment, they were locked together; gasping as they struggled.

Next, the brute went staggering back, and his right arm hung limp by his side; the knife dropped from his fingers, and he began to utter little whimpering sounds. Rollison went in fast and savagely again, giving himself time to smack right and left to the jaw, and put his man down. Then, he turned, to find his cabby coming from the cab, mouth wide open, eyes rounded in disbelief when he saw the pair of jungle beasts.

"Caw!" he breathed.

"Pardner," said Rollison, breathing very hard, "it's none of your business, and you'll be crazy if you get yourself mixed up with it. But if these guys happened to get locked in the trunk of your cab, you'd qualify to belong to the State of Texas."

As he spoke, he was bending down over the first man he had knocked out. He ran through his pockets, then moved him so that he was stretched out on his back.

"You could even take them to hospital," went on Rollison, "and say you found them two or three blocks away."

"Bud," said the cabby, "it's none of my business, but you've got something. Cheese! They might gimme a reward for hospitalising the guys, eh? Okay. Give me a hand with them."

The job took a fraction under two minutes; the first man was put in the taxi's trunk, which Rollison knew as the boot; and the other on the floor in the back of the taxi. This man's right arm was broken, but the other did not seem to be badly hurt. The cabby was in a tearing hurry to get off.

"I'll be back," he flung over his shoulder. "Don't go far, bud."

Rollison watched him drive off, smiled, and said in a curiously mild voice:

"Bless your stout heart. Bud."

Then, he turned towards Number 48, putting into his own pockets everything he had taken from the men's.

The street door was still ajar, and Rollison stepped in and closed it. The house was silent. Light came from a ceiling light in the hall, which was narrow with a flight of stairs leading off at one side. Men's hats, some plastic raincoats and some oddments were on a hallstand. The door by the side of the hallstand was closed. A black card hung from a nail, reading: Ask Here. He didn't, but started up the stairs. They were carpeted, but nothing could stop them from groaning. He kept to one side of them, close to the wall; that way, he kept the sound to a minimum. As he neared the next landing, he saw that passages led both ways; short, narrow, ill-lit. At the end of each was a door, and beneath one door a strip of light. He approached the door which was in darkness, taking out a penknife which had several odd blades. One was a skeleton key. He used it, swiftly, the sharp, dexterous turns making little sound. He knew that he was piling risk on risk; things he could get away with in London, where he knew the police, might run him into outsize trouble in New York; but this wasn't the time to be faint-hearted.

He opened the door.

Silent darkness greeted him.

He closed this door and approached the other, and then went to the lighted apartment; as he drew nearer, he heard the drone of radio or television, and didn't think it likely that Brian Conway or the others were sitting back and having fun.

They might have the radio on, to drown any sound.

He used the key again, as deftly as before, but this time opened the door much more cautiously. Light came through; and beyond was another open door, showing a television set and the feet of a man and a woman sitting just out of his line of vision.

He went out.

The two doors on the next floor led to empty rooms.

On the third floor, one door looked to be in darkness, the other had light round it, but no sound came. Rollison used the key again, quickly but very cautiously; for this was the top floor of the building - if he judged it rightly, the third floor back. There was nowhere else for Valerie to be.

Valerie Hall didn't like any of what happened.

From the time they had bustled her into the taxi, on Broadway, she hadn't liked it at all. There'd been too much haste, and the grip on her arm had been much too tight. When they'd got in the taxi, Conway had sat one side of her and the stranger the other; and both men had held her arms, and looked ready to clap a hand over her face. They had been breathing hard and interested in something happening in the street, which Valerie hadn't noticed.

She was more scared then ever, in case anything had happened to the man Rollison. But she didn't spend much time thinking about Rollison, then, except to remember what he had advised her to do.

She relaxed, and sat back.

The others relaxed, too.

The narrow-faced man had called an order to the driver - 48 something street. Now, they travelled very fast. At first other traffic was close on their heels, some cars actually passed them. Lights were vivid at first, but soon became much less powerful. Valerie could look down streets which were almost in darkness. As the lights dimmed, her hope dimmed too, and her fears rose. Rollison's first advice had been best - stay indoors.

She knew that she couldn't have done so.

Now and again, the man with the narrow face looked round, obviously to find out whether they were being followed. Conway's manner had changed, and now he kept patting her hand, and saying:

"It's okay, Val, it's okay."

She didn't like his touch; or him.

She liked the narrow-faced man much less.

He had been waiting in the restaurant, where Brian Conway had said that he would be, solitary, dark, oddly frightening; a man who looked as if he could be really bad.

They had talked a lot about 'dough' and 'Wilf', keeping their voices low. Valerie had fought hard to make sure that she didn't raise hers. She had been determined not to hand over the diamonds or the money until she had seen Wilf, but at heart she had known that she might have to; she would do anything to give Wilf a chance. Conway had tried to make her less adamant, as if he was frightened of the narrow-faced man. Perhaps he was.

Valerie had told herself that she hadn't a hope of gaining her point, that she might even be putting Wilf in great danger by holding out.

Then, abruptly:

"Okay, okay," the narrow-faced man had said, "you can see him. Okay."

So, they'd left the restaurant.

Valerie hadn't seen Rollison anywhere near.

Twenty minutes later, the narrow-faced man opened the door of a room in a dark, gloomy building a long way from Times Square. There was a smell of stale cooking, and a sickly smell of paint. The stairs creaked. There was dust on window-ledges and on the banisters. She was in front of both men, and they came up single file. She could easily have screamed. The sight of lights beneath some of the door didn't reassure her. She was hopelessly confused; there was the hope of seeing Wilf as well as fear that she would not, fear that this was simply a trick.

The narrow-faced man had opened a door with a key, and thrust it back.

"Listen, you're on the level, aren't you?" Conway asked, in a timid-sounding voice. If he knew the man, would he be so timid? Was there any chance that she and Rollison were wrong about him? Or was this just part of the act?

The narrow-faced man gave a one-sided grin.

"Sure," he said, "this is on the level. It's on my level." He slid his right hand to the inside of his coat, and before Valerie realised what he was doing, he produced a gun. He didn't point it at her or at Conway, just held it casually. "Sure," he repeated; "you don't have to worry. Inside."

"Listen, you said . . ." Conway breathed. Was he genuinely frightened?

"I don't have to listen," the narrow-faced man said. "Inside."

They went in.

The only light was the one which the man had switched on. There was no sound. When the door closed it seemed to shut them off from the world. They were in a tiny lobby, with arched doorways without doors leading off it in two directions. The narrow-faced man manoeuvred so that both of them were in front of him, and then said:

"Put on that light."

Conway obeyed.

He was nervous - wasn't he? It wasn't just pretended.

Valerie looked round a sitting-room, with some armchairs, a threadbare carpet, a table against the wall. The only hint of luxury was in the big television which filled a corner. Compared with the suite at the Arden-Astoria, this was a slum apartment. It was empty; of course it was; but Valerie couldn't stop herself from saying:

"Where - where is he?"

"You want to see your brother?" sneered the narrow-faced man. "Okay, you can see him." He went to a small bureau in another corner, and picked something up, brought it across and thrust it into Valerie's face. "That him?"

It was an enlargement from a coloured snap of Wilfred Hall,

taken while he had been here in New York. It couldn't have been a better likeness. Smiling, nice-looking, strong, healthy, and radiating a kind of confidence. He was their father all over again, the true son of the man who had built up the Hall millions half-way round the world.

Valerie hadn't seen him for three months.

She looked up into the narrow face. Had Rollison seen her then, he would have recognised most of the emotions which chased one another.

"I want to see him in the flesh," she said, very firmly, "and until I do . . ."

The narrow-faced man said smoothly, nastily: "Don't get me wrong, sister. You're not seeing your brother until we're ready to show him, and that's not now. Where's the dough and where are the jewels?"

"I'm not giving them to you until I've seen Wilf," Valerie said. By some miracle, she managed to keep her voice steady, to sound determined. She stared at the man, defiantly. She felt her heart thundering with such fear that she could hardly breathe, but didn't drop her eyes. "You said"

"Val," muttered Brian Conway, "take it easy; don't make him mad."

"That's good advice," the narrow-faced man said; "why don't you take it? And you'll sure make me mad if you don't hand over. Come on, sister."

He put out a hand; it was long and narrow - and dirty. Even palm upwards, the tips of dirty nails showed. Yet it was very steady, with the fingers curled slightly upwards, like a claw.

"Val, I told you not to come," Conway muttered; "I warned you what would happen. You'd better hand over; this guy doesn't care whether you're a girl or not; he wants the jewels. Don't be crazy, Val; don't get yourself hurt."

She blazed up at him.

"You snivelling little coward, what do you think you are to tell me what to do? Why don't you do something, instead of standing there looking as if you'll melt into the floor? If there's one thing I can't stand it's a coward! That's what you are, a hopeless, helpless, snivelling coward; if you had half Wilf's guts you'd wade into this beast." Her eyes were blazing and her fists were clenched and she shook them at Conway, not at the narrow-faced man, who had first been startled, and now began to grin as if this was a great joke. "Why, I've seen braver men than you crawl" Valerie cried, and took a step forward as if to strike Conway. "Why don't you do something?"

Conway thrust out a hand defensively.

"Val . . ." he began.

Then, she sprang round towards the narrow-faced man and struck the gun out of his hand.

He was taken completely by surprise, and as the gun fell and he backed away, Valerie jumped towards the door.

8

MOUSE INTO LION

THE door, in fact, was some way off; Valerie had to go through an arched doorway to reach it. She had a good start, for the narrow-faced man was off his balance when she actually reached the archway, and Conway was gasping:

'Val, be careful, Val!"

That didn't deter her for a moment. She reached the actual door which led to the passage, and as she did so, the narrow-faced man called:

"Stop right there!"

"Stay where you are or he'll shoot," Conway cried in desperation.

He sounded as if he knew it was true.

Valerie didn't stop to think whether it was or not, but snatched at the door-handle; and as she did so, her foot caught against a rug and she pitched into the door. Thus she lost her only chance even of reaching the locked door. The narrow-faced man moved, swift as a fox, and reached her before she could pick herself up. He had the gun in his right hand, but didn't use it. He put an arm round her waist and lifted her clear of the floor; she was so small that it didn't need a strong man. Then he half-dragged and half-carried her back to the inner room, where Conway stood pale-faced and shaky of limb, moistening his lips, and looking anywhere but at Valerie.

The narrow-faced man dropped Valerie on to a couch, and when she tried to scramble up, he slapped her face.

"Don't do that," Conway muttered.

A moth fluttering against the light would have attracted more attention.

The narrow-faced man pulled Valerie's handbag from her fingers, opened it, and emptied the contents on the table. Small leather boxes which might be jewel-boxes fell out. He looked at these with glinting eyes; and with gloating satisfaction, He opened one box, and a slender diamond pendant winked and shimmered up at him, all colours of the rainbow scintillating about the room.

"Sure," he said softly; "that's real ice." He closed the box and slid it into his pocket, then put the others into his pocket without looking inside them. Next, he picked up a roll of dollars which were held together with a rubber band. He didn't trouble to take the band off when he tucked them away.

There was nothing else of value in the bag.

The man looked at Valerie's ears.

The ear-rings looked like a thousand dollars.

"Okay," he said, "take 'em off."

Valerie was now sitting upright on the couch, with her knees close together, and her hands folded tightly in her lap. Her lips were pressed into a thin line, as if she was trying to hold back her fury. Her eyes glittered as brightly and as hard and dazzling as the diamonds.

"If you want these," she said defiantly, "come and get them."

"Val, don't" squeaked Conway.

She showed no sign that she had heard him, but glared at the narrow-faced man. He stood with one hand at his hip for a moment, the other in his pocket. He grinned. He had a small mouth, and when he smiled it opened just enough to show even teeth set in a small jaw.

"The pocket Venus wants to mix it, does she?" he said

nastily, and stretched out his hand. "Don't argue, gimme."

She didn't move.

"Val!" came from Conway as a muted shriek.

The narrow-faced man stopped grinning; obviously there was an end to his admiration for feminine courage. He went forward, hands thrust out and fingers claw-shaped; as if he were going to choke her before wrenching the ear-rings away. She hadn't room to get up, just sat there with her hands clenched now, fury keeping fear away.

Then, Conway cried:

"Stay where you are. Don't move!"

The man with the narrow face stopped, as if a current had been switched off. He looked round, at the mouse turned lion - and Conway had a gun in his hand, and was covering him. Conway's face was working, but his hand kept steady.

The man with the narrow face spun round.

"Keep back!" cried Conway, and there was sweat on his forehead and a wild look in his eyes. "Keep back, or ..."

The other made as if to jump at him; and Conway fired.

And on that instant, the door opened.

Rollison had the door open, making hardly a sound, when he heard the shot from Conway's gun. Until then he had heard two or three shouts, and sensed the frightening tension; so the shot didn't really surprise him. As he went in, as if lightning carried him, he felt a sharp and agonising fear: that Valerie Hall had been hurt.   Then, he saw her.

She was on a couch, rearing away from the narrow-faced man who was staggering with his hands held chest high, and an awful expression on his face. It wasn't just pain; it wasn't just rage. It was the look of a man who was passing out of this life into another; and the next world seemed so full of horror that he could not bear to go.

He clawed at his chest.

He crumpled up.

Brian Conway stood staring at him, the smoking gun still in

his hand. He didn't speak. He licked his lips, and the sweat was like beads on his forehead and on his upper lip.

Valerie stared down at the narrow-faced man.

"You killed him," she said chokily, "you've killed him."

There was a short, sickening pause; and then Conway gasped: "If I hadn't he would have killed you. I had to do it, I had to!" He took a step towards Valerie, hands stretched out pleadingly. "Val, you know that, he would have killed you; look at the rest of the things he did. He would have killed you; I tell you, I had to kill him. Val! Don't look at me like that; I was only trying to protect you."

Valerie didn't speak.

Rollison watched all this from the arched doorway; nothing that either of the others did or said suggested that he had been noticed.

"Val," Conway said, moistening his lips again, "we've got to get away from here. Don't just sit there; we must move. No one need know we've been here, if we hurry. Let - let's get the diamonds and the money and then ..."

He broke off.

Valerie stood up, slowly. The shock was fading. She began to look as if she could understand something of the forces which drove Brian Conway on; as if she could understand what made him mouse one moment, lion the next, and back to mouse in the twinkling of an eye.

"All right, Brian," she said quietly; "but supposing someone comes to see what's happened."

"They - they won't." He wasn't as sure as he tried to make out. "You - you don't poke your nose into other people's business when you live in this part of New York; you just lock your door and pretend you heard nothing. We - we've got time. I - I'll get the jewels, and ..."

"You could even make sure that he's dead," said Rollison, mildly.

He moved forward.

Conway spun round, mouth opened as if to give a scream

which wouldn't come. His right hand made a flapping move towards his pocket and the gun, but he didn't actually touch it.

Valerie cried: "You!" in a funny little voice, and tried to step over the man on the floor. She caught her heel in his coat, and stumbled; then suddenly she crumpled up, crouching on the couch with her face in her hands, while Rollison moved swiftly towards her, and Brian Conway looked on.

Rollison went down on one knee, and felt for the shot man's pulse.

The man was dead.

He had little in his pockets except the stolen jewels and money; his own wallet contained forty-seven dollars, and several letters addressed to Al Cadey, at 48 East 13th Street; this address - so this was Al Cadey. The bullet had gone through the heart. Blood was already spreading over his cream shirt and his pale brown linen jacket. In death, his mouth was slack and he looked very ugly.

"We - we've got to get out of here," Brian Conway muttered. "I - I don't mind, but if the police are called and they find Valerie here, they - they - they'll" He couldn't finish.

Valerie was like a statue.

"Val," Rollison said, "shake out of it." He wanted to search the apartment, but knew that Conway was right, the first job was to get the girl away; and he couldn't trust Conway to take her. "Val, it'll be all right; we'll find Wilf." His words had no effect on her, and he pushed the dead man aside and then bent down, took Valerie by the waist, and lifted her. He carried her to the door, and Conway followed hastily, switched out the light, and went ahead. He was breathing very heavily; fear was at his heels all the time.

Rollison began to whistle softly.

Half-way down, Valerie's body went limp and she no longer held herself stiff. Rollison lowered her, gently. She didn't speak, just looked at him, then walked ahead.

In his pocket were her jewels, her money, the dead Al

Cadey's keys and wallet, and the letters to Cadey.

They reached the street.

The taxi was waiting a few doors along.

The time might come when the taxi-driver would be a liability, not an asset, but it was impossible to brush him off now. Brian Conway muttered some kind of scare line, but Rollison called quietly to the cabby:

"Hotel Commodore, this time."

"Commodore?"

"Please."

"If it's okay with you, it's okay with me," said the cabby. He seemed impressed by Valerie, and he was smiling happily. "Girl friend with the wrong boy friend," he said; "what do you think of that?" He was smoking, now, while they all sat in the back of the taxi, and he took them swiftly to the front entrance of the Commodore. "Say, bud," he went on, "were you good for that bad boy friend or bad for the good girl friend?" The gust of laughter which followed nearly split him in two.

"You bet," said Rollison, and grinned back. He produced another twenty-dollar bill. "When I want you, where can I find you?" he asked.

The cabby whisked a card into his patron's fingers.

"Ring this number and just ask for Sikoski," he said. "You got the name? Sikoski. Don't worry, it's written down. You don't have to worry about those two knockouts," he added. "I fixed them good. You sure you don't want me any more tonight?"

"No, thanks."

"If it's okay, it's okay. Be good to the bad girl!" He burst out with fresh laughter as he drove off, while Rollison watched him, smiling faintly, then turned towards Conway and the girl. They hadn't moved. Rollison took Valerie's arm, and they walked towards Madison Avenue. At the first chance when out of sight of the Commodore, he called another taxi, and within five minutes they were back at the Arden-Astoria.

The night had not changed.

It was a little cooler, that was all.

As they went in, it was nearly three o'clock. The same staff was on duty. An elevator car stood empty. Rollison jauntily, as befitted his appearance, Conway briskly, Valerie smoothly, they crossed the lobby and then went up to their floor. The same Floor Clerk wished them good night, and gaped after Rollison, as if she noticed that his ten-gallon hat had been trodden in the dust.

At Valerie's door, Brian Conway said miserably:

"Val, I can't tell you how sorry I am about the way I let that guy push you around, but - okay, okay, I was scared. I knew he was a killer; you can always tell a killer. If you'd let Mike and me handle it, it would have been okay."

"Would it?" asked Valerie. There was no spirit in her voice, now; just a flat weariness. "Would you have found Wilf? Wilf," she repeated as they went in, and Rollison closed the door. "Oh, Wilf."

"I'll find him if it's the last thing I ever do!" Conway burst out.

Rollison didn't interrupt; not then, and not when Mike Halloran came hurrying from the bathroom. At sight of Rollison, he backed away, and stood gaping.

"It's been a hell of a night," Conway told him; "every thing's gone wrong, and I - I killed a man. It was self-defence. I don't know what he would have done to Valerie if I hadn't, but she seems to think ..."

Valerie said: "I just want to find Wilf, that's all." There were tears in her eyes. "Mr. Conway, I - I'm grateful, really, I - I know you did it for me."

"Val!"

She turned away and went into the bedroom, without closing the door behind her. They heard her moving slowly towards the window.

Halloran said: "Brian, obviously this ain't no place for us." He didn't even ask who Rollison was, but took Conway's arm and started to lead him towards the passage door. Conway's expression suggested that he did not think Rollison would let him go, but Rollison didn't say a word; and didn't break his silence until both men were outside.

Then, he moved.

He reached the telephone, and as the operator came on, said: "Bell Captain, fast," and held on for a split second. A man answered briskly. "Bell Captain.... Two men are coming down now; they came in with me and Miss Hall ten minutes ago. I want you to detain them until I call again or come down, please." He didn't wait for a response, just rang off, took a card from his pocket, and lifted the receiver again. He could see Valerie in the doorway, watching him as if bewildered while he studied the card - which had some pencilled notes. The operator answered. "Can you get me the Milwest Hotel, please?" Rollison said. "Sure, I'll wait."

He waited.

Valerie came in, much more briskly than she had gone out; tears gone and hope coming back.

"What are you doing now?"

"Checking," he said. "If Conway gave a phoney address, I'll follow him." He stretched out a hand and Valerie came towards him, without saying a word. He slid his arm round her waist in a friendly, comforting way. "I don't know why Conway shot Cadey, unless he believed Cadey was going to kill you, and wouldn't stand for it. We'll find out." He heard the operator of the Milwest Hotel, and spoke more briskly. "Do you have a Mr. Brian Conway staying there, please? ... Oh, fine, thank you. ... Room 87, that's fine. ... And Mr. Michael Halloran. ... The next room. Thank you very much." He rang off, and looked down at Valerie; then suddenly moved his arms and lifted her effortlessly, with both arms. "You know," he said gently, "you're very sweet." His kiss was a brother's kiss. "Now get some sleep. Wilf will be all right. While they've Wilf, remember, they have a chance of getting more of your millions, and they'll hold on to both Wilf and the chance like leeches." He wasn't sure, of course - he couldn't be sure, for the victim of kidnappers was often a liability while alive; and it was easy to pretend that one who was dead was alive. "Don't worry about it, Val, and in the morning we'll make the next move. For tonight I'm going to sleep in a chair outside your door, and I'm not taking no for an answer."

She didn't say no.

"I'll put your jewels in a safe deposit box downstairs," Rollison went on, and gave her back the money which he'd taken from Cadey's pocket.

Half an hour later, he went into her suite again, and saw her lying in bed, small and pale and heavy-eyed, as if the shocks and excitements and the fears that lingered had drawn the spirit out of her.

He closed the door, and settled down for the night, quite sure that if anyone tried to get in, he would be alert on the instant.

He had three questions on his mind.

First - where was Val's brother?

Second - could he and Valerie be traced to 48 East 13th Street?

Third - what should he do with the body in his own suite?

He thought of a fourth, too: of the hipless young man who had been so savagely beaten up. He pondered a lot about that, before he dozed off.

When he woke, it was to the urgent ringing of a bell; he didn't know where and he didn't know what bell. It was dark and shadowy, and until he saw the single light burning in the bathroom and sending some light in here, he forgot where he was. As soon as he remembered, he stood up. His mouth was sticky and his eyes heavy; it might be four o'clock or ten. The ringing of the bell seemed to become more and more urgent as it went on. Bells often did. The bedroom door was closed, but if this rang much more Valerie was bound to be disturbed. Rollison stood up, and yawned; but his head was clear, and that told him that the morning was well on.

Brr-brr-brr.

"Stop that damned row," he said, irritably, and strode to the door. He didn't open it at first. There was no way of being sure that the caller was a friend. There were many awkward possibilities, too: that the body next door had been found, that he and Valerie had been seen in 13th Street and that the dead man had been discovered there. Or...

Standing to one side, and thus out of the range of anyone with hostile ideas and a gun, he opened the door.

With a finger poised to ring again, Brian Conway stood outside. Unshaven, unwashed, clothes rumpled, eyes scared.

"Let me in," he breathed, "let me in!" and he glanced over his shoulder as if frightened out of his wits.

9

TALK OF DUTCH HIMMY

No one was behind Conway.

Rollison stood aside to let him in, and saw no one in the passage; more, he heard no one. Yet Conway was in a state of jitters which set his teeth a-chatter. Rollison closed the door and turned to look at him long and intently, while Conway fought for self-control, and finally managed to say:

"I - I'm being followed everywhere."

"Don't you like your friends?"

"Friends?" ejaculated Conway. "They're no friends of mine! I - I wish to heaven I'd never offered to help Val. I'd be a happy man if I'd never heard of her!"

"So you would," murmured Rollison.

"Look where it's got me," muttered Conway. "I don't have a minute's peace. Nor does Mike Halloran. He - he takes it better than I do, but I can't help it if I get scared. I tell you I can't help it if I get scared!"

"That's right," said Rollison. "Who was blaming you?"

"You were! I could see it in the way you looked at me, as if I was a worm. And the way she looked, last night, after I'd shot that man. Anyone would think I was a pariah - but if it hadn't been for her I wouldn't have taken the chance. Sup - sup - supposing I'd missed. What do you think he would have done to me?"

"Let's not even guess," said Rollison, mercifully.

He glanced towards the bedroom door, and saw that it was opening; but it didn't open wide. It meant that Valerie was not only awake, but interested enough to listen without revealing the fact that she was there. He didn't let her down, but said to Conway:

"Now take it easy. And how about some coffee?"

"Sure, I - I haven't had any breakfast."

"Then how about some?"

"Oh, I couldn't eat," said Conway, in a tone of revulsion. He gulped as he dropped into an easy-chair, and took out cigarettes. He lit one without offering to Rollison. "How - how - how's Valerie?"

"Sleeping it off, I hope."

"I've done more for that girl than I've ever done for anyone in my life," Conway muttered. "Why, I might even die for her."

"They won't kill you for that job," Rollison assured him, "even I could help to prove that it was self-defence. Unless we all get hooked on a complicity charge," he added thoughtfully. "Then we'd all die. I . . ."

Conway shuddered.

There might be a lot of things that Rollison did not know about him or about anyone else, but one thing seemed certain: Conway was in an acute state of funk. If this was just to fool Rollison, it was his best acting yet. The way he kept glancing at the door, the way he started when there were sharp noises from the street or along the passage, was ample proof of that. He watched as Rollison went to the telephone and ordered breakfast for two and coffee for three, and then said:

"If Valerie wakes up, she'll be ready for some coffee. Now, what's been worrying you? Who's been following you?"

"D-D-D-Dutch Himmy," Conway blurted.

He brought the name out as if he was saying 'the Devil himself. He was still very pale, and his voice wasn't steady; the cigarette quivered whether it was in his mouth or in his fingers. "You - you wouldn't know about Dutch Himmy, but he

- he's terrorised parts of New York. They don't come any worse. He's the man who kidnapped Val's brother, and - and the man I shot was one of his gunmen. He rang me up this morning, and he said - he said I wouldn't live to see the day out."

"He couldn't have been trying to frighten you, could he?"

"He means it, he always . . ." Conway broke off.

"How do you know so much about the gentleman?" asked Rollison, mildly. "Aren't you and Mike Halloran such law-abiding types?" Nothing in his manner or his tone suggested that he suspected Conway of complicity in the kidnapping and the ransom.

"I - I get around," Conway muttered; "and anyway, you've only got to read the papers. They all talk about Dutch Himmy; he - he's a man the cops want but can't trace; they don't even know who he is. He's got them on the run, and - and when he puts his finger on a man, that's the end."

"It might be the wrong end for Dutch Himmy one day," said Rollison, brightly. He took out a whisky flask and, without a word, handed it to Conway. Conway grabbed; the whisky gurgled. He gasped as he handed the flask back.

"Now, what else did he say?" asked Rollison, still mildly.

"He - he asked me if I knew who you were," said Conway, and there was a kind of defiance in his manner; almost a kind of courage. "When I said no, he told me. You should have heard him! He said he wasn't going to stand any argument from a goddam limey; he didn't care if you were the finest private eye in the world, he - he'd cut you into pieces and send you back home by parcel post. That's what he said" cried Conway. "I'm only telling you."

"And what did you tell him?"

"I said - I said you were good!"

"Hmm," said Rollison, sadly; "it would have been much better if you'd persuaded him I was a decadent piece of the English aristocracy and not worth two cents, but never mind." He couldn't understand Conway, unless the man was genuinely frightened. If this was just a tale to fool him, the Toff, why talk of Dutch Himmy and go into detail? Rollison surveyed Conway long and thoughtfully, as if he was trying to find out what made him tick. Then, abruptly: "What else did Dutch Himmy say?"

Conway gulped.

"It can't be any worse," said Rollison.

Conway shot an agonised glance towards the door.

"He - he - he said that if he didn't get all those jewels and the money Val had by tonight, he - he'd - he'd cut off Wilf Hall's right hand."

There it was; the threat with all its starkness, all its brutality; the thing which was in keeping with what had happened, with murder and savagery and ruthlessness. It was threat enough to make Rollison stand very still and quiet; and obviously it had terrified Conway, who looked towards the door again, as if hoping desperately that Val hadn't heard.

The door opened, and Valerie came in.

She was flushed, and her eyes were bright; too bright. She wore a dressing-gown of royal blue, which set off the beauty of her hair and her eyes. She was holding the gown together at the breast, and at the neck. She came in quite slowly and deliberately, and looked from Conway to the Toff and back. At last, she said:

"If it's like that, then I'll have to hand over everything. Everything. Go back and tell this Dutch man, please. Tell him I'll give him what he wants, provided he doesn't hurt Wilf."

Conway began to get up.

Rollison watched everything about them both with keen interest, weighing one thing against another. The contrast between the unshaven Conway, with his bleary eyes and quivering lips, was startling against Valerie's morning loveliness. She was as calm as he was agitated, and gave the impression that nothing would make her change her mind.

"I don't know where he is; he said he'd telephone me again this afternoon," Conway said. "I had to leave Mike at the hotel, in case Dutch Himmy wants to give a message before then. Are you - are you serious? You will hand the jewels over?"

"Of course."

"Even if he doesn't release Wilf first?"

Valerie glanced at Rollison, as if she expected a protest from him; but he kept his peace.

"Yes," she said; "I don't see how I can help myself. I can't take any risk that Wilf will be mutilated. After all, the diamonds aren't all that valuable." Then suddenly she clicked her tongue, showing real emotion for the first time. "Oh, what a beastly thing to say! If it meant every penny I'd got, I'd pay it for Wilf's safety."

"But don't tell Dutch Himmy that," put in Rollison, as if urgently. "It might give him ideas. Is that everything, Conway?"

"Isn't it enough?" Conway almost shouted.

"One's always looking out for the last straw," murmured Rollison. "I"

There was a tap at the door.

Rollison went to open it, with just as much caution as he had before, but this time he needed even less, for it was a white-jacketed waiter with a heavily laden trolley. He wheeled it in.

Rollison went to the corner of the passage, and made sure that no one was watching. The daytime Floor Clerk sat near the elevators, and everything was quite normal. Rollison went in the other direction. Near his room there was a narrow service staircase, and a service elevator alongside it. He went back to Valerie's room, where the waiter was setting out the breakfast, and said:

"I'll be back in five minutes."

He went out again, hurried for one of two big laundry baskets on the landing, and pushed it into his own suite - his first visit since he'd left here looking like a Texas colonel. The body of the man who had died in Valerie's arms was still in the wardrobe where he had put it; wrapped in the plastic water-and-blood-proof coat, sheets and blankets. A little blood had come through. He put on his gloves, lifted the heavy body into the big laundry basket, covered it with dirty linen, and then wheeled it back into the passage. The waiter was at the door of Valerie's room; Rollison left the basket where it was, and slipped back out of sight. The waiter came past with his trolley, but seemed to think nothing of the laundry basket as he went into the service elevator. After he'd gone down, Rollison pushed the basket to the elevator, waited until a lighted sign said: Ground Floor, and pressed; the elevator came up at once. There was ample room for the basket. Rollison pushed it in, and closed the door. He'd hardly moved away before the basket rose slowly out of sight with its grisly burden, summoned by some hapless member of the staff. If the body were found quickly . . .

It might not be.

Rollison went back, took off his gloves, washed his hands, and made sure that there were no obvious signs of blood anywhere; the room wouldn't stand up to a "thorough police search, but there was no reason why the search should start on this floor.

He went back to the next room.

Valerie and Conway sat at a square table, eating. It was immediately apparent that they were at the stage of repletion. One piece of toast was left. The two bacon-and-egg plates were so clean that they might have been wiped round with a piece of toast. The conserve dish was empty. Rollison observed all this, and then very slowly shook his head.

"I'm glad no one's been put off food," he said, earnestly; "it shows a reasonable state of health. Couldn't spare a cup of coffee, could you?"

"Oh, what pigs we are!" exclaimed Valerie. "We just ate without thinking. After all, I didn't have a bite to eat last night." That was by way of explanation, not excuse. "We can soon send for more, and . . ."

"I'll go down to the coffee-shop for some," said Rollison, "after Conway's gone. You lock your door, Val; and don't let anyone in except me or the police."

Conway jumped, spilling his coffee.

"Police?"

"Well, they might find us," observed Rollison, reasonably. "You can't go spilling blood and bodies all over New York without some kind of a protest. Finished eating?" He stood over Conway until he finished his coffee, and then escorted him to the door. Whether Conway was bluffing or not, he was jittery; was perhaps in danger from this Dutch Himmy for falling down on his job.

"Will - will you stay here?" he asked, at the door.

"Tell your pal Dutch that I'll be here, there and everywhere," said the Toff, brightly; "he may not have known much of me before, but that's no reason why he should stay in that state of blissful ignorance. After all, he started it." He paused, and as Conway moved away, went on very softly: "And tell him not to hurt Wilf Hall. Tell him that if Wilf is hurt, I will personally break his, Himmy's, neck. Make sure he knows I mean it."

He went in, and closed the door.

He turned, to see an unexpected picture. Valerie, standing by the table, was in that moment positively dewy-eyed. Rollison had seen the look in the eyes of many young and impressionable damsels, and it never failed to give him pleasure; in these later days it seldom failed to surprise him, either. Here was a girl looking at him in a way which mingled adoration with admiration; and Valerie Hall knew exactly how to mingle them both. She was a natural.

"It's time you got dressed," Rollison said, firmly.

"Yes, I will," said Valerie, but didn't move. "You really meant that, didn't you?"

"What?"

"If this man Himmy hurts Wilf, you'll break his neck."

"I'll have a damned good try."

"In spite of his reputation, and using gunmen, and - things like that."

"You can be so careful that every time you go downstairs

you count the steps," said Rollison, "and break your neck when looking out of a window. Don't get ideas, Val. Get dressed, and be ready to do anything I ask - quickly. If we have to stall with those diamonds, we have to stall, but we needn't ask for trouble, and you're leaving the Arden-Astoria for somewhere Dutch Himmy doesn't know about. Lock yourself in until I come back, won't you?"

"Yes," said Valerie, and added with a stubborn note that he couldn't fail to hear: "But nothing is going to stop me from trying to buy Wilf's safety. I know all the arguments, that the more you pay the more the kidnappers ask, but I can't help it. If you go to the police, or if you do anything that makes Dutch Himmy hurt Wilf, I'll never forgive you."

"You know," observed the Toff, sadly, "you ought to have been born a boy."

10

FRIEND IN NEED

ROLLISON went back to his own suite, and for the first time since he had stepped into the Arden-Astoria, felt that he had time to breathe. He did not make the mistake of thinking that this happy state of affairs would last for long. Facts were facts. Dutch Himmy might be a degree worse than Legs Diamond or Al Capone. Certainly he knew what he was about. Brian Conway might or might not like working for him. That didn't alter a situation which was likely to get rapidly worse.

It was no longer possible to handle the case alone.

Among the most disturbing possibilities was that Valerie Hall might decide that she was more capable of handling the situation than anyone else. If she once got the bit between her teeth, she would set a hard pace. She had now come to the conclusion that only by paying Dutch Himmy could she help her brother, and Rollison shrugged the thought off.

He went to the telephone in his sitting-room, sat down at ease in an armchair and, after some study of the dialling system and exchange numbers, dialled a number and was answered with bewildering promptitude by a bright young woman who said:

"Day's Personal Investigation Bureau, can I help you?"

"Bless you," said Rollison, warmly.

"What did you say?"

"I asked to speak to Mr. Day."

"You did not," said the girl, the last word rising several notes and ending in a hint of laughter. "Who is calling, please?"

"Richard Rollison, from London."

"Oh, sure, I could tell you were English; but . . ."

There was a pause, a sharp exclamation, and then she went on in a very different tone, echoing: "Mr. Richard Rollison?"

"Yes."

"The Toff in person?"

"As soon as I have an hour free, you and I are going to get together," said Rollison, earnestly, "luncheon or preferably dinner and a show and the rest of the evening exactly to your liking. You're the first person out of New York's teeming millions who even knows how to pronounce the name. Is Cyrus in?"

"Oh, sure," she said, eagerly; "he'll be in for you. Hold the line just a minute, please."

She went off, carrying her excitement with her. It was soothingly satisfying, and helped to place the affair of Dutch Himmy into a little better perspective; not all people were so utterly indifferent to the Toff. He did not have to hold on for long, just time enough to tell himself that if he didn't eat soon there would be a hole right through him, when a man's voice sounded in his ear. A fine, deep, American voice, which carried heartiness and warmth and obvious pleasure.

"Say, Rolly, is that really you?"

"Cy, it's I," confirmed Rollison. "Hungry, unhappy, helpless, in need of a friend and a great big build-up. How are you fixed for time?"

"For you, I've all the time in the world," said Cyrus Day; and that was generosity itself, for he was the executive head of the largest inquiry bureau in four continents. "What time is it now? - just after eleven o'clock. Say, will you have lunch with me?"

"Alone?"

"If that's the way you want it."

"Please, Cy. Half-past twelve all right?"

"Fine. Would you like to come to the office, or shall I come to you?"

"Let's work out the best thing to do," said Rollison, settling down in his chair and resigning himself to another hour and a half of sorrowful longing for food; but his spirits could hardly have been higher after such a reception. "Are you taking notes?"

"My secretary will, if you'll hold on. Miriam!" Day called to someone in the office, "go to that extension and take some notes, will you?" He paused. "Okay, Rolly, go right ahead."

"Thanks," said Rollison, cheerfully. "First, there was a beating-up in 49th Street just off Broadway last night - young chap was kicked and badly knocked about, I think. Will you trace him for me?"

"Sure."

"Second. I've a young and pretty and rich young woman with a mind of her own, in trouble in New York, and I'd like to get her away from the Arden-Astoria to some place where she'll be watched properly, and where we can make sure that she doesn't do anything silly - like trying to come to terms with Dutch Himmy, for instance."

He paused.

He heard two distinct sounds at the other end of the telephone; one from Cyrus Day, the other from Secretary Miriam. The pause which followed was long and unquestionably pregnant. Then the girl Miriam said in a whisper: - "Did I get that right? Dutch Himmy?"

"Rolly," said Cyrus Day, "did you say Dutch Himmy?"

"That's what I'm told."

"So that's what you're told," echoed Cyrus Day. "You just hold on a minute. Legs!" he roared, and nearly deafened the Toff. "Legs, come here, will you? ... Legs, you know Mr. Rollison, don't you?"

"Sure," a man said, faintly in the background.

"Fine. Rolly, where are you staying - the Arden-Astoria?"

"Suite 552."

"Thanks. Legs, you take anyone we've got to spare with you,

and go to the Arden-Astoria right away and keep an eye on Mr. Rollison. It appears that he's mixing it with Dutch Himmy, and we don't want Dutch to get hurt, do we? You keep tag on Mr. Rollison, and have the other operator check everywhere in the hotel, to see if there's any legman of Dutch's about. If there is, tell me who it is and how many - tell me everything, and don't lose any time about it. You heard me?"

Faintly, there came the response.

"I'm on my way."

"Hallo Rolly," Cyrus Day said, back into the telephone. "Be sensible for once and give Legs time to get there so that you're covered all the way. You'll need to be. You can do two things, right now. Order your funeral service or go back to London." There was still a chuckle in his voice. "Or you could if you were any other man! Now, what's this about a girl you want to hide?"

"I just want her somewhere safe."

"You have a word with Legs, as soon as he arrives," said Day. "Have him take the girl to the Belle Hotel, out on Riverside Drive. That's where most of our operatives live if they're not married, and she'll be as safe there as she will anywhere in New York. She'll get good service, too; it's small, but we look after our clients. Leave all decisions to Legs. If he says you shouldn't go with her, don't go with her. Understand that?"

"Perfectly," the Toff said humbly. "I'm sorry that I brought dynamite with me."

"You didn't bring dynamite, you brought the hydrogen-bomb plant," Cyrus declared. "What other little things would you like me to do for you?"

Rollison chuckled.

"Something misfired in East 13th Street, out near the East River Parkway - I don't know whether a thing called Cadey - Al Cadey - has been found yet. And two men should have been taken to hospital by a cabby named Sikoski."

"Two hospitalised - not Dutch Himmy's men?" That possibility seemed too much even for Cyrus Day; he almost screeched.

"I wouldn't know," said Rollison solemnly.

Day said: "Okay, I'll see what I can do; but I don't know that I'll have all the information you want by the time we meet for lunch. Don't come here; I'll meet you at Keane's."

"Chop house?"

"Sure."

"That sounds like real food, and I've never been so near malnutrition," declared Rollison. "Cy, there's just one other little thing you might start for me."

"Little?" echoed Day, suspiciously.

"Oh, I don't think it's very much. Give me a build-up. Can you? Tell the news-hounds I'm here, give them some of the balderdash about being Britain's Ace private eye, East Enders in terror - you could even tell them about my trophy wall. Didn't you have some pictures when you were in London? That'll fetch 'em, if anything will. And a picture of Jolly, the last of the gentlemen's gentlemen - he sends his good wishes, by the way."

"Good wishes is exactly what I need," Day said, feelingly. "I think I understand. You'd like Dutch Himmy to get the build-up?"

"Would it do any harm?"

"No," said Day, slowly. "No, I guess not. Especially if I say that you always work in the closest co-operation with the police." There was another pause. "Sure, I'll fix it, Rolly; maybe it will be a good idea."

"Fine. Charge all expenses to ..."

"Oh, forget it. I owe you at least a hundred thousand dollars for the way you helped me in London, and ..."

"To Wilfred and Valerie Hall," finished Rollison.

"Hall," echoed Cy Day. "You got that, Miriam? Wilfred and Valerie - hey! Rolly! Do you know what you're saying? Wilfred Hall? Why, he's just bought the Atyeo Building, right here. The third highest in New York. He"

"He's just got himself kidnapped by Dutch Himmy," said the

Toff.

This time the pause was a long one; and this time, when Day broke it, it was in a gruff and worried voice; there was no more nonsense, nothing else that was even slightly flippant. That more than anything else told Rollison how highly Dutch Himmy was rated as a bad man.

When Rollison finished his talk it was twenty minutes past eleven.

He telephoned Room Service for a sandwich and some coffee, then looked in on Valerie. She was still in her dressing-gown, her face was rosy, her hair a wispy dream, the bathroom door was open and the mirror dulled with steam. So she hadn't planned a sudden sortie on her own.

"Val," Rollison said, "I'm going to have lunch with the best private inquiry agent in New York. He's on our side. He wants you to leave very soon, and go to a smaller hotel where his operators can keep an eye on you all the time."

She looked at him owlishly, and considered.

"Very well," she said; "but I don't want there to be any mistake, Mr. Rollison. I'm not going to let anything stop me from helping Wilf."

"It's the only job that matters, and one way is to make sure you don't run into trouble," Rollison told her. "As for helping Wilf - if we have to come to terms with Dutch Himmy, my friend is the best go-between. He can find out exactly what the kidnapper wants, and he can make everything else easy. Well, easier."

Valerie, looking as kissable as a debutante, nodded as with great wisdom.

"Very well," she conceded again. "So long as we understand each other. Do you say this private inquiry agent thinks he can look after me - I mean, save me from being hurt or kidnapped? I suppose it is possible that they might try to kidnap me."

"Possible, yes," Rollison said. "They're more likely to frighten you, hoping you'll do what they want, which is probably get a lot of money. If they'd wanted to kidnap you, they'd probably have tried before. It looks as if they think they've the better chance with Wilf a captive and you a free agent. If anyone in New York can protect you from any rough stuff, this agent's men can."

"Oh, good," said Valerie, and added naively: "If he can protect me he can protect Brian Conway, can't he?"

"What?" exclaimed Rollison, and for once was bereft of words.

"Oh, I'm quite serious," said Valerie, calmly. "I don't like to think that Brian is so frightened because of me. You may be right, I suppose, and he may be in the scheme, but I'm not positive. And whether he is or not, he's scared stiff, and it's my fault. After all, he did kill that man for me, didn't he?"

"That's how it looked," agreed Rollison, faintly.

"Then I owe him something in return," insisted Valerie. "I know you would have saved me from anything more unpleasant, but at the time of the shooting, Brian Conway didn't know that, did he?"

"Er - no. But, Val . . ."

"I don't want to appear stubborn," went on Valerie, in her steeliest, sweetest voice, "but I really do mean this, and I don't mind what it costs. It isn't only out of a sense of fair play, either. I rather like Brian Conway."

There was a touch of defiance in her manner when she said that; enough to show that she meant exactly what she said. And just now, Rollison decided, it was wise to humour her.

He left her to get dressed.

His greatest anxiety was to get her safely to the hotel which Day had recommended. He realised that he was suffering from a mild attack of delayed shock, not due to what had happened, but to the obvious seriousness with which Day took Dutch Himmy. Only a man with a really black reputation could have made the inquiry agent take such swift and decisive steps.

Well, Cy was a friend in time of need. . . .

Soon, Rollison let Valerie leave, with 'Legs' - who proved his identity beyond any doubt.

An hour afterwards, Rollison stepped out of a taxi and into Keane's Chop House. He knew it, of old. He did not expect to be recognised by the manager, and welcomed, but he was. He glowed. Cy Day was waiting for him in a corner, with a Tom Collins in his hand. Day was a big, pale-faced man, well-dressed, looking more like a financial tycoon than the world's top private eye. He was putting on weight, and when he shook hands, showed that he wasn't losing his grip.

"It's okay," he said. "I've just had a message from Legs; she's safely at the Belle Hotel. She'll be all right. That is, she'll be as nearly all right as anyone can when they've crossed swords with Dutch Himmy. Let me tell you about him."

"First, let me eat," pleaded Rollison, and he had his way.

11

THE VICTIM

THE Toff had eaten.

He felt as if he now needed a long sleep, but knew that there was no likelihood that he would get one. He had only to dwell on the things which Cy Day had told him about Dutch Himmy to wake up. These things had the quality of nightmares. It was the kind of situation which had happened before and would happen again, but this was different in a number of ways. In the past, the identity of the criminal had been known; only proof against him was needed. This time, 'Dutch Himmy' was simply a name. There were even people who believed that he was no more than a name, just a huge hoax invented to fool the police and to make far lesser men tremble.

No one could be sure.

Many of the crimes of New York were laid at the door of Dutch Himmy; including murder. It was not good even to listen to some of the things that had been done in his name. The girls maltreated and the children corroded with drugs, the men beaten up until they were good for nothing but a mental hospital or a home for cripples.

Many who were said to have worked for Dutch Himmy had been caught, some executed, others sent down for long terms of imprisonment, but none had given a clue to the identity of Dutch Himmy himself. The police had come to believe that the reason was simple: they didn't know.

But more and more people knew of the man and were frightened of him.

"Nothing at all surprising about the way this man Conway is behaving," Day said, in that deep, attractive voice. He had clear brown eyes and the smile of a preacher. "Himmy's turned plenty of brave men into cowards - and sometimes it's the only sensible thing to be. If Conway's on his pay-roll and fell down on the job - by letting you get around, or killing Cadey - then Dutch Himmy would frighten the wits out of him, and he'd be desperate to make the next job go right. I don't handle any case which I know leads back to Himmy if I can avoid it, Rolly, and when I do it's only to protect a client. I never go after Dutch."

Rollison, drawing at a cigarette, slowly screwed up his eyes and said:

"Oh. Thanks."

"I hope you won't force this too far," Cy Day said, cajolingly. "I'll come as far as I can with you, but it's really a police job, and that's the truth of it."

"Think the police will find Wilf Hall?"

Cy Day said very slowly and very quietly: "No. I don't think anyone will find Wilf Hall until Dutch Himmy wants him found. Whether he'll be found alive or dead is another matter."

Rollison didn't speak.

Day found a kind of grin.

"All right, all right," he said; "you sit there and laugh at me; but, take it from me, you're the fool. Dutch is everything I've told you. If you act on my advice, you'll just try to come to terms as soon as you can."

"Hum," said the Toff.

"From what I can gather, Wilf Hall's sister has come to that conclusion already," went on Day.

"Yes, she has," agreed the Toff. He stubbed out his cigarette and lit another. He wasn't exactly smiling, although his eyes held a glint that might have been of amusement, and his lips were slightly curved. "You could be absolutely right, Cy."

Day gave a deep chuckle.

"If that isn't just like you! You listen to a considered opinion from the one man in New York who knows all the angles, and you concede he might be right. Well, I suppose I ought to be grateful for that." He was still sardonically amused. "And I don't forget that against all the advice of the experts in London, you did the Kingham job your way, and it came off. So I'm prepared to listen to reasoned argument."

"Not argument," said the Toff. "Neither logic nor reason, not even a hunch. Now that really is something to be grateful about! Just a - er - feeling?"

Slowly, admiringly, Cy Day shook his head, and ash fell off his long cigar on to his pale grey suit.

"That you could be taking Dutch Himmy a little too seriously," murmured the Toff. "One can get into a frame of mind, my Cy. Himmy's here and Himmy's there, Himmy's victorious everywhere, and he gets home before the chase has started. Not even a clue as to his identity?"

Firmly, Day said: "No."

Softly, the Toff said: "Liar."

Day chuckled again, and took his cigar from his lips, but didn't look away.

"If I knew, I would tell you. But you're holding a press conference at my office in half an hour, and you might pick up a name or two from the newspapermen. They make a guess a day as to Dutch Himmy's identity. If you really want to stick your neck out, ask the Night Telegram man. Named Dando. He's the one who hates Dutch Himmy most, because his own brother got too close - and died. But if I wanted to see Wilf Hall again, I'd wait for further word from this man Conway, and then do whatever Himmy says."

Rollison didn't speak.

"I'll do everything I can to protect you and the girl, but I can't guarantee a thing," went on Day, earnestly. "That's the way it is, Rolly." He put the cigar back to his mouth, and continued almost wonderingly: "I wonder if this is the way Dutch Himmy will fold up. You've just one advantage that we haven't got over here."

"Thanks. Tell me."

"He won't have the faintest idea what to expect next," said Day, wonderingly. He snapped his fingers for the bill. "We'll have to be on our way; it wouldn't do to keep those newspapermen waiting, would it?"

They got up.

In the taxi going to Day's offices, in the fabulous Atyeo Building, Day said mildly:

"Dutch Himmy's said to have eyes and ears everywhere, so I don't trust a soul. But right here, where we can't be overheard, I'll tell you one thing: I'll give you all the help you need, unofficially. I'll tell you where to go for help, and I'll pull all strings I can. But the Cyrus J. Day agency can't come in as itself."

"Understood," said Rollison, gratefully. "Thanks, Cy. Any news of that young chap who was beaten up? Or Cadey?"

"Might be, when we get to the office," said Day.

Soon, they drew up outside the Atyeo Building. It was between Fifth and Madison Avenues, and deceptive. At first sight the block seemed like any other in the heart of New York; high, of course, but that was all. Then, one started to look towards the top, and it began to be truly fabulous. Vast stretches of stone and glass rose skywards, until one got a crick in the neck. In fact, it was impossible to see the top from this side of the road, or even from the other side, unless one was some distance off; it vanished into the sky.

Rollison saw it from a distance, and gaped as they drew nearer.

"And Wilf Hall bought this?"

"His American company did," Day said. "And what a place! It rates third to Rockefeller Centre and the Empire State Building. Ten thousand people work in it; you can buy anything you want in the shops in the underground concourse; you can be born and cremated, you can do a clip-joint, a high-class night-club or go to church. It's a village within a village and town within a town. I wouldn't like to tell you how many million dollars it's worth."

"I wouldn't mind a few shares in Wilf's American company," said Rollison, as if in tones of envy. "Or meeting a few of his fellow directors. Could you fix it?"

"The one thing you want to do is keep away from them," Day told him, "and don't breathe a word to anyone about the kidnapping. If it gets out, it could do a hell of a lot of damage to the Hall shares - and that could cost some people all the money they've got. It would cost all the shareholders a pile, too. Don't say a word, just keep it right under your hat." "Yes, sir," Rollison said.

Cy Day had been taken seriously. There were fifteen reporters and five photographers waiting in the outer offices of the agency's sumptuous apartments. They had all been given hand-outs and photographs of the Toff's trophy wall, in London; the wall on which he hung the souvenirs of those cases which had ended with him alive. He described several. The one they liked most was the story of the top hat with a bullet hole in it; next, the cuckoo clock which cucked a bullet large enough to kill. They were fascinated by his tale of a hangman's rope, on show at his Mayfair flat simply to impress all callers; and they loved all they heard of his man, one Jolly.

They wanted to know what had brought him here, and if he expected to add any trophies.

"Good Lord, no," said Rollison, as if horrified. "Not the idea at all. I'm here just to say hallo to a few friends, and look at New York again. Love the place."

They were satisfied.

Except for a tall, lean, hungry-looking man, who stayed behind when the rest had gone. He was Dando of the Night Telegram.

"Mr. Rollison," he said, "there's one question I'd like to ask you without the others present. Will you object?"

"Glad to try to answer," said Rollison, pleasantly.

Dando didn't go on at once, and Rollison studied him closely. His eyes were a curious light grey. When he had seen him for the first time, Rollison had judged him as a man with a chip on his shoulder; but it was more than that. It was grief for a dead brother and the desire for vengeance; and it was easy to believe that these things had become an obsession in this man. His jaw was bony, his cheeks sunk in, the pale grey eyes had a hard glitter.

"Have you come to find Dutch Himmy?" he asked, abruptly.

Rollison said politely: "I beg your pardon?"

Dando didn't repeat the question, but just looked Rollison up and down, and turned away. He spoke over his shoulder, almost as an afterthought.

"If that's who you're after, come and see me," he invited. "Any time."

The spacious outer offices of the agency were empty except for the debris. Miriam, a pretty and nicely matured brunette, was collecting the ash-trays, most of which were filled with ash and cigarette ends, and two blondes and a young man with red hair were collecting glasses and putting bottles away. Cy Day took Rollison into an inner sanctum, which had all the sumptuousness of a Hollywood director's or a Wall Street miracle man's. Seeing the way Rollison glanced round, Day said:

"We have to have something to impress the clients."

"If they're all as impressed as I, you must have a lot of clients," said Rollison, with feeling. He stood in front of an easy-chair. "What does one do in a thing like this? Sit, fall or lie down?"

"Suit yourself - I always recline." Day moved to a padded chair behind a mammoth desk, on which were a variety of telephones, a terrifying looking box-like instrument, as well as some simple things like pins, pens and paper. "Well, you went over big."

"You put me over. Thanks."

"I've had a press conference that lasted half the time yours did, in spite of the best liquor in town," Day assured him. "You made your mark, Rolly. What did Dando have to ask?"

Rollison told him.

"Hmm," said Day, thoughtfully. "Well, I always believed that if anyone gets Dutch Himmy, it will be Dando - and if Dando really wants help, he couldn't have it better than from you. All the same, I wish Wilf Hall had called on some other private eye; I prefer to keep you in one piece." Day opened a folder on his desk. "Now, let's see." He chuckled. "That taxi-driver of yours, Sikoski, is quite a character. He didn't take those two hoodlums to hospital, he dropped them down-town, in the Bowery. The police found them, and took them over. One had a broken arm, the other a sprained ankle, and neither will be much good for some time."

"Would they serve Dutch Himmy?" inquired Rollison, hopefully.

"No one's said that they do, and they haven't opened their mouths," Day told him. "There's no report of a body being found anywhere in New York last night - if that's what you meant by talking about this thing called Cadey."

"Chap might just have been knocked cold," murmured Rollison, apologetically. "Pity; he wasn't at all nice. Name of Al."

Day sat still behind the opulent desk.

"Al Cadey," he echoed, and his tone and expression changed. "I was waiting for you to say it was Al. That's it, Rolly, you're really fighting Dutch; there's no more doubt about it. Cadey's just out after serving three years for a Dutch Himmy job," Day drummed the desk with his fingers unhappily; "and if Cadey's gunning for you, you'd better have eyes back of your head as well as the front, and some just above the ears." Suddenly, he grinned. "Anyone would think that I was trying to frighten you, wouldn't they?"

"Yes, wouldn't they?"

"But you know me," Day said. "I hope! Now, what else have we got? Report on Brian Conway - nothing known. He's here on a British passport, if that's useful to know. Michael or Micky Halloran - he's a different proposition, now. He's just out of the can; served five years of a seven-year sentence for fraud."

"Ah," breathed Rollison. "No uranium."

"He's been out nearly six months, and nothing's known against him in that time," said Day. "Dutch Himmy had only just started when Halloran went inside, but I don't know that that tells us anything." He scanned the papers in front of him again. "Ah, the guy who was beaten up. Well, it could have been a lot worse for him, I guess. He was taken to hospital, but they didn't keep him in. Van Russell, 110 West 67th Street. That's an apartment block. Middle-income group. He's thirty-four, comes from Pennsylvania - farming country - an accountant, and he knows Wilf Hall because he's an executive of the accountants who handle Hall's account. Seems just a nice little guy. Another thing. He has a sister, name of Julie, who was going to marry Dando's young brother. You won't be surprised that Dando and Van Russell see a lot of each other." He took a photograph from the folder, and pushed it across the desk. Rollison had to ease himself out of the encompassing arms of the chair to get it. "Recognise him?"

Rollison studied the rather thin, pleasant face of Van Russell. It was a good picture of the 'hipless' man he had seen last night, and there was no possibility of a mistake. Russell looked as if he was going thin on top, and he hadn't the biggest of chins. Some would say there was a lack of something; virility? He had a lazy look, but looks could be so deceptive.

"Thanks, Cy," Rollison said again. "I think I'll have a word with Russell before I do anything else." He gave his quick, attractive grin. "Think it's safe?"

"Nothing's safe."

"Did he say why he'd been attacked?"

"Didn't open his mouth," Day said. 'Well, if you mean to go on, you've got all my good wishes, Rolly - and maybe you'll get a lot of help from many unexpected places. No one has any love for Dutch Himmy."

"Thanks," said Rollison.

"And I've made a start on helping you," Day told him. "I've hired you a regular cab. I've had the driver screened, and he's okay, and he knows New York like no one else except other taxi-drivers. He's outside waiting for you now and he's yours for keeps."

"Cy," said Rollison, "you make it too easy."

"Easy!" choked Day.

Rollison grinned.

"What's in a word? Cy, there are some other jobs you can do a hundred times better than I."

"Name one, and I'll prove you wrong."

"Don't make my head swell," chided Rollison. "First - trace Wilf Hall's movements in the last few days, and especially after he left the Arden-Astoria for the airport."

"Will do."

"Find out if anyone would like to do him wrong."

"Everyone likes Wilf Hall," Cy said. "But - well, okay."

"And see if you can find out anything about a man named Mark Quentin." He described the man who had died at Valerie's door, and went on: "Who he worked for, all that kind of thing."

"I'll do all that," said Cy. "That everything?"

"For now, yes, thanks."

Cy Day pressed buttons and Miriam came to guide Rollison out, through the big room which looked sleek and shiny again, to the elevator, down to the street level, to the swing doors - and almost into the arms of Bud Sikoski.

12

VAN RUSSELL

"Blow me down, pardner," boomed Sikoski, "if it ain't the Colonel from Texas. I'm sure glad to meet you, Colonel!" He extended a great hand. "Sitting in the taxi just now I was asking myself a question. Bud, I was asking myself, I wonder if you'll ever see the Texas Colonel again. That," explained Bud Sikoski, "was the question I was asking myself."

"And what did you answer?" inquired Rollison, politely.

They had reached the yellow-and-red taxi. This was a street where no parking was permitted but ten minutes waiting was winked at by the cops.

They got in.

"To be honest with you," said Sikoski, "the answer I gave myself was just like this, Colonel - I don't know, Bud. Maybe I would, I said to myself, and maybe I wouldn't. What do you know about that?"

"I'm making up my mind," Rollison told him. "West 67th, Bud, please." They started off. "I hear that you had a better idea about the two hoodlums."

"Not better," said Sikoski, earnestly. "Just as good, though, and quicker. You should have seen me unload them, yes sir! And they call jet aircraft fast! You having yourself a good time in New York, Colonel?"

"It was all right last night," said Rollison; "today's been a bit slow."

"Well, what do you know about that!" breathed Sikoski. "New York slow. Colonel, I can't allow that to happen, I really can't."

He trod on the accelerator....

Faint and exhausted, Rollison looked up at the building marked 110-112 West 67th Street. Compared with buildings in most cities of the world, it was mammoth and tall; here, it was middling size. It looked fairly new. There were swing doors and several elevators, a gloomy hall. With Sikoski waiting outside, double-parked and promising to keep driving round the block if he was moved on by the police, Rollison went in. It was just a square hall, with four elevators, all automatic and without a lift-boy.

Rollison went straight up to the seventh floor, then walked along a narrow passage to Apartment 79. Everything was clean and well-decorated; it had no luxury, but it was all right. After a pause, the door was opened by a small woman; little more than a girl. She had a nervous expression and her features were so like Russell's that it was obvious that they were brother and sister.

This must be his sister Julie.

She greeted: "Good afternoon."

"Good afternoon," said Rollison. "Is Mr. Russell in?"

"He has someone with him right now."

"I won't keep him long," said Rollison. "I'm a friend of Wilfred Hall."

Julie Russell hesitated. She had pale blue eyes, and she still looked rather nervous; timid was perhaps the better word.

"You'd better come in," she said; "I'll go and see if he'll see you. What name, please?"

"Rollison."

She seemed to repeat the name under her breath as she let him in, and then went off. A door opened, and Rollison heard voices; one of them seemed to be familiar, but he couldn't place it. He looked about this room, with its good furniture and excellent taste. Two walls were dark red, one white, one a shaded white and pale blue. Did the timid little creature who had opened the door have such good taste as this?

The man whose voice he recognised said: "What name did you say?"

"Rollison," answered Julie.

"Is this guy English?"

"Yes, I think so."

"Well, what do you think about that?" said the man, and a chair scraped and footsteps sounded heavily. Next moment, Dando of the Night Telegram came from one of the other rooms, bending his head in order to miss the archway. He was grinning one-sidedly, but that didn't make him any the less gaunt. "Now isn't this a coincidence? You and me both here."

Rollison said mildly: "It must be an affinity."

"Or it might be a mutual interest in Dutch Himmy," Dando said. "There's a guy in here who hasn't much love for Dutch Himmy right now. Come and shake him by the hand; it makes three of us." He led the way, and Rollison went into a large, airy bedroom, past the timid girl, Julie, who slipped out without a word.

"Van," said Dando, "come and meet the second best private eye in the world - according to Cy Day."

Van Russell was sitting up in bed.

Nothing Day had said had prepared Rollison for the bandaged head, the swollen and discoloured right eye, and the fact that his left arm was in a sling. His left eye was clear enough - velvety brown and appealing - and his right arm hadn't been hurt; the hand on the white bedspread looked lean and sinewy. He was giving a one-sided grin.

"Hi," he said.

"Hi," said Rollison.

"Now that's over," Dando said, "let me tell you something, Mr. Rollison-Toff. Van is a friend of Wilf Hall. Wilf Hall's gone away for a few days, his secretary won't say where. His sister's in New York, and you know something about that. Van was so worried about her he kept an eye open last night and he followed her from the Arden-Astoria. She was with a guy he doesn't know, and they joined a guy he does. A gun-slinger for Dutch Himmy, named Cadey. Heard of Al Cadey?"

"No," said Rollison.

"I wouldn't like to earn my living guessing when you're lying," Dando said, "I'd be on the hunger line most of the time. These two hustled Valerie Hall off last night, but she's back at the Arden-Astoria now. Know what happened in between?"

Rollison didn't answer.

"Even you can't answer 'no' to that one and expect to live," Dando said. It wasn't exactly a sneer, but it wasn't far short. "Toff, let me tell you something. Van thinks that Wilf may have been kidnapped by Dutch Himmy, and that there'll soon be pressure on his sister to pay a big ransom. Is that what you think, too?"

Rollison said mildly: "If you weren't a newspaperman, I might begin to talk."

Dando moved towards him, and stood very close. It was almost possible to feel the burning intensity of his eyes, to understand something of the torment which consumed him.

"Listen," he said; "I live for one thing - finding Dutch Himmy and breaking him into little pieces. That's my beginning and my end. Any story I get that might help, I use. Any time it would help to keep quiet, I keep quiet. Even Van knows that."

Russell was leaning back on his pillows.

He had a nice smile, even though a third of it was hidden by a bandage. He didn't give the impression of timidity, as Rollison had half expected. He looked very small, lying in bed; boyish. It was almost a surprise to think that he was in the middle thirties. His one visible brown eye glowed. He had nothing of Dando's intensity, but might possess a lot of Valerie's stubbornness.

"What do you know?" Rollison asked him.

"Well, for one thing, that Wilf asked you to come over from England," said Russell. He had a quiet voice. "He told me about it. He told me that he was worried about Valerie coming, but she insisted on it. He also told me that he was nervous about an attack on him or on Valerie, and although he didn't say so, I guess he'd already had some trouble."

"With whom?" Rollison asked.

"Could be with anyone, could be with Dutch Himmy," said Russell. The voice was either tired or lazy; perhaps he had been a long time coming round from his beating-up; perhaps he wasn't really himself again yet. "For one thing, he closed up his house in Westchester, he used to commute most days, and went to live at the Arden-Astoria. He didn't say so, but I guess he felt safer there." Russell paused, and then went on: "Mr. Rollison, I can't tell you very much - but I think that Wilf found himself up against Dutch Himmy, and didn't have time to do all he wanted to do about it. He knew he couldn't stop his sister from coming to New York, so he hired you to watch her. He had to find someone who didn't know the risks of tackling Dutch Himmy - no one on this side would have taken the job on and be absolutely trustworthy."

Russell stopped, and his eyelid drooped.

Rollison said: "You don't know it was Himmy; you're just guessing."

"That's right," Russell said. "I'm just guessing. But I know there was trouble. I know that Wilf went to three of the big agencies in New York, including Day's, and they wouldn't take his commission. I can think only of one man who would stop them from taking Wilf Hall's money - and that's Dutch Himmy. I don't know what the trouble was, but I know Wilf had to go it alone."

"Hmm," said Rollison, and took cigarettes from his pocket. He shuffled them from the packet. "There's one little thing I just didn't realise."

"I don't understand you," Russell said.

"I thought there were police in New York." Rollison held out the cigarettes to Dando, who was smiling tight-lipped; he took a cigarette, but Russell waved the packet away.

"Whatever the trouble was," he said, "Wilf wouldn't go to the police."

"Sure?"

"He said as much in so many words."

"Need that stop us?" asked Rollison, and took a light which Dando offered. "From going to the police, I mean?"

"It would stop me," Russell said. "But then, I'm just a friend of Wilf Hall."

Rollison grinned.

Dando looked less tense, now that he was smoking. The atmosphere in the room had eased considerably, too. Russell relaxed on his pillows, and looked thoroughly uncomfortable. His closed eye would look like a sunset over the Nile in a day or two; and Rollison found himself wondering how much damage had been done to his scalp.

"Where do we go from here?" asked Dando, suddenly. "If Cy Day threw that party for you, Rollison, then he might be prepared to help against Dutch Himmy at last. I don't say I blame him, I don't blame any of them, because Himmy could ruin them, but - well, it's bad when a man can make an agency like Cy Day's lay off him. Cy a friend of yours?"

"Business acquaintance," Rollison said.

"Some friend," Dando said, and sat smoking in silence. Russell seemed mildly amused, but in fact might just be tired out. Both men were waiting for a move from Rollison.

The presence of Dando complicated it for him; and he had already learned most of the things he had expected.

Dando took the cigarette from his lips.

"Here's the guy with all the big ideas," he jeered.

"Unpopular ideas," murmured Rollison.

"What makes them that way?"

Rollison said, dreamily: "It must be something in the English climate. Will one of you jump on me whenever I go wrong in my guesses?"

"Jump is one word," Dando said.

"Land easy." Rollison's voice was still dreamy. "First, Valerie comes to New York at precisely the time that Wilf was kidnapped; so, the kidnappers probably knew she was on the way, and timed the snatch to coincide."

He paused, but neither of the others corrected him.

"Second, Dutch Himmy wants ransom of a kind from Valerie, and at the moment he's playing with small chips. Expressively called chicken-feed, I've been told. Wilf is worth the Atyeo Building, plus a lot more millions of dollars in New York. The Hall Trust and the Hall Corporation in Great Britain are worth a medium fair slice of London. We won't test our arithmetic - we don't have to, in order to know that the hundred thousand dollars which was first demanded was just the opening play."

He won his sensation. Dando jumped up from his chair, Russell raised his sound hand and moved his other involuntarily. They eyed Rollison as if he were crazy.

"Are you sure of that hundred grand?" Dando demanded.

"Yes. They used a man named Conway and another named Halloran to work as go-betweens. They did some talking, and Dutch Himmy is supposed to have settled for all the loose cash that Valerie had with her, plus a few oddments of jewellery. Say sixty to seventy thousand dollars' worth at most."

"Not on your life!" Dando breathed.

"Dutch Himmy wouldn't think in peanuts," Russell said, softly. "This Conway - you heard of him?"

"No," said Dando; "but Halloran - Halloran was in the can for a job Al Cadey did."

"Cadey," said Rollison, softly, "is the man supposed to have settled for the peanuts on Dutch's behalf."

"Cadey," breathed Dando. "It could be. Yes, sir, it could be that he was ready to settle - that he tried to double-cross Dutch Himmy. Cadey's body was taken out of the East River, about an hour ago, and there was a bullet in his chest. I was told about that just before I came to see Van. If Cadey was trying to muscle in, Dutch would snuff him out - sure, that would explain a great deal. But it's only the sparring, Toff;

Dutch Himmy wouldn't do all this for a hundred grand. He might"

The newspaperman broke off.

"Jeb," said Russell, mildly, "we interrupted Mr. Rollison. He was going to suggest an unpopular idea, and I'm still interested."

Dando stubbed out his cigarette, and then lit another.

"Aren't we all?" he asked.

Rollison said: "Well, you haven't thrown me out yet. How is this for a play? Dutch Himmy knows that Valerie is here in New York. The timing is so perfect that we can be sure of two things: either he means to work on Wilf by threatening Valerie, or Valerie by threatening Wilf.

Either way, we're guessing. But Valerie must be vital to him, so if we were to kidnap Valerie and let the world know of the snatch" He broke off, with a self-deprecatory smile, and when the others just gaped, went on disparagingly: "After all, I was in London yesterday, and we're retarded over there. I know it might mean bad trouble for Wilf, but wouldn't it put Dutch Himmy's plans out of joint?"

13

CAUSE FOR ALARM?

DANDO began to smile, and Russell began to grin. They stopped gaping at the Toff, and looked at each other. It was Dando who said, wonderingly:

"I'm beginning to understand what Cy Day meant. Sure. Dutch Himmy's snatched Wilf, and maybe he thinks that he can now make Valerie do what he wants, but he can't if he's lost track of Valerie. If she's just hiding, that's one thing; if she's been kidnapped..."

He began to chuckle.

The Toff said, mildly: "I don't know how much you know about the crime life of New York, but do they all let Dutch Himmy get away with it?"

"Come again," said Dando.

"Is he the only bad man who matters? No competition, I mean?" said Dando.

Now, Russell's one visible eye took on a glowing delight. Dando lit another cigarette, shot smoke towards the ceiling, then answered very softly:

"No, sir. There are others. And if it were spread around that one of the other parties has snatched Valerie, just to muscle in on Dutch Himmy - do I understand you?"

"You understand me."

"Toff," said Dando, earnestly, "don't go back home. If you

survive this day, stay in New York. We can use you. How soon can you make Valerie disappear, and where will you take her?"

Rollison stood up.

"Soon," he said. "Somewhere." He moved to the door, smiling amiably at them. "Cy Day is looking after Valerie at the moment; if you keep a check on him you'll find out when she's vanished."

"Here, Toff!" cried Dando.

He wanted to learn more. He failed to, then. It seemed to him and to Russell that one moment Rollison was standing there in the doorway, and the next he had vanished. In fact, all the normal processes had been carried out, and he had even had time to smile at the timid girl who looked so much like Russell. He let himself out, and the luck was with him; the elevator was at this landing. He was at ground-floor level before Dando reached the front door of the apartment.

Sikoski was reading a book of strip cartoons with great intentness, spelling out the words which ballooned out of the characters' mouths. At sound of Rollison's approach, he folded this artistic gem, thrust it into his pocket, opened the door and started the engine, and he did all of those things in the same flash of time.

"Okay?" he asked.

"Okay," agreed Rollison, solemnly.

"Okay," said Sikoski. "Where now?"

"Arden-Astoria," said Rollison, and promptly changed his mind. "Make it the Commodore."

"So long as it's one at a time."

At the Commodore Hotel, Rollison told the cabby to go back to his garage and wait for a call which wouldn't come for at least three hours, and then went blithely into the hotel. In five minutes he had arranged, via the Bell Captain, for a drive-yourself car to be brought round to the back entrance of the hotel; it was promised in twenty minutes. He next made his way to the telephone booths near this entrance, and put in a call to an old, old friend, who now had an American wife and owned a farm in New Jersey, not far from Jersey City. The call came through in some seconds under two minutes, and a clearly English voice said:

"Hallo, there."

"Tim," said Rollison in his gentlest voice, "you don't remember a guy named Rollison, do you?"

There was a pause; and then the flood.

"Rolly!" boomed Tim Mellish. "Is that you in the flesh? Mary said she'd heard something on the radio about you being in New York, so she, was right. Wonderful! Where are you? When can we meet? How"

"Easy, Tim," pleaded the Toff, and so won a respite. "Do you and Mary still believe in taking risks?"

"Depends what they're for?"

Very briefly the Toff gave him the gist of what he wanted; and he won a respectful silence until he stopped, when Tim Mellish promptly and quite nonchalantly said:

"Glad to help, as always. When will you bring her here?"

"How long will it take me to drive from New York?"

"Well," said Tim, "I don't know, exactly; it depends what the traffic's like through the city. Once you're this end of the Holland Tunnel it isn't too bad; say about an hour and a quarter from there. Allow two hours in all, for safety. Now, listen . . ."

He gave precise instructions, and soon the Toff rang off.

He went outside, at once. A sleek black Cadillac was already there, with a chauffeur. He gave Cy Day's name as a reference, paid two hundred dollars down, and was permitted to drive the car under the chauffeur's instructions. After the first few seconds, the chauffeur stopped instructing him, for it was obvious that Rollison was a natural at the wheel.

"Where shall I drop you?" he asked.

"Anywhere will do fine," said the chauffeur, "but if you're going near Park and 36th, that would be just right for me."

Rollison dropped him as he requested.

There was plenty of parking room out here, and Rollison

soon pulled up near a cigar store, and went to a telephone. This time, he rang the Belle Hotel and asked for Valerie. It occurred to him uneasily that she might already have run into trouble; she hadn't, for she was still there, and wanted to see him.

"That couldn't be better," said Rollison; "we want the same thing, Val. How do you like it there?"

"I hate it," Valerie said, firmly; "I feel that I'm being watched all the time. Is there any news from Conway?"

"Not yet," said Rollison, "but there's news of a kind. You are being watched all the time. I've got to get you out of the Belle Hotel without anyone knowing where you're going." He paused to give her a chance to speak, but she didn't take it. "Will you walk out, in twenty minutes' time, and head towards Riverside Drive, near 77th Street? I'll be waiting for you in a black Cadillac, and as I slow down, I'll open the door. You hop in."

"All right," Valerie promised, without a moment's hesitation.

Rollison went out, and took the wheel, made immediately for the west side, and was tangled in traffic at Broadway. Traffic was much busier here on a Sunday than it was in London. He was thirty minutes instead of twenty getting to the rendezvous, and for the first time he was really worried.

Valerie was walking along, on the other side of the road.

Two men were a little way behind her, and it was easy to believe that they were Cy Day's. Rollison swung the car round in a U turn, and stopped alongside her. She was ready on the instant, and got in, slamming the door. He put his foot down and the car shot off; and as it did so, a green Buick pulled out of a row parked twenty yards behind, and moved after him.

Here was Cy's agency working at speed.

Rollison swung into 77th Street.

If he had luck at the lights, he would shake the car off quickly; if he was out of luck, it would take a long time. He glanced at Valerie, who seemed slightly flushed with excitement;

that was all. He judged the lights nicely, sent the Cadillac forward and swung into Tenth Avenue, took a chance and turned into the next street, heading for Broadway. It was one way, and his way. On Broadway he went down to 72nd Street, then turned towards Riverside Drive again; and he could no longer see the green Buick which had started the chase. He went fast on to the Hudson River Parkway, and still didn't see the Buick; but he did know how thorough Cy Day's men would be; probably they had had a second car after him. He headed north; and at the first chance, near the pale, graceful span of the George Washington Bridge, took a sharp left turn, and was soon heading south again.

"I suppose you do know where we're going," said Valerie, almost tartly.

"Oh, yes." He smiled at her, but kept his gaze on the road. "To some friends of mine in New Jersey. English husband, American wife, three little Mellishes, and all modern conveniences plus life on the farm. You'll love it there, you won't be watched, and we'll be able to play bat-and-ball with Dutch Himmy."

He didn't look to see, but it was easy to imagine the expression in Valerie's big eyes.

"What are you planning?"

He told her, briefly.

"Oh," she said, vouchsafing neither approval nor disapproval. She was thinking it over, and that was as much as he could expect. He reached the signs reading Holland Tunnel and soon they were at the approaches to the entrance, with about five hundred other cars. They vanished out of daylight, and the tunnel, with its yellow lights and the red rear lights of all the cars and the sidelights of cars approaching from the other direction looked like a preview of hell. Valerie peered about her as if fascinated. The tyres rumbled, the tunnel seemed to be filled with a great wind. They dared not slacken speed, and seemed to be travelling much faster than the limit which was written in tall letters on the sides: 30. At different places, they saw policemen standing on raised platforms built into the wall.

On and on and on.

"Doesn't it ever end?" asked Valerie.

"It did the last time I was here," Rollison said. "Have a nap, if you're tired."

She startled him by bursting out laughing.

Soon, they saw the beginning of daylight; and soon the traffic spread out, and they were passed by some cars which seemed to fly, and they passed others which were going at a fair speed. New York was behind them, they were in New Jersey on the west side of the Hudson River, and according to Tim Mellish, an hour and a quarter's run from his farm.

Rollison didn't see the green Buick in the mirror.

He pulled into the side, to allow all the traffic to pass him; and everything in sight did pass. If he'd been followed, would the pursuing car have gone on?

A fantastic ribbon of road stretched out in front of them. He needed to slow down, and to make sure that he was on the right one; if he once got off it, he would lose much more time than he could afford. They came to the city limits of a little town, and he pulled into the side of the road, and took out the map.

"Won't be long, now," he promised Valerie; "be patient for a little longer." He offered her a cigarette, and she took one; he lit it for her, and then studied the map, oblivious of Valerie and the passing traffic and everything that was happening. It wasn't until he felt the wind steal into the car and glanced up, that he realised that anything odd was happening.

Valerie had opened the door.

She was getting out.

14

SWEET REASON

"VAL!" Rollison exclaimed, and grabbed her.

In another second, he would be too late. Even as it was, he might be. He caught her arm and she tugged to get free, and when she couldn't, twisted round and struck out at his face. Her fingers just missed his eyes, and involuntarily he closed them and slackened his grip.

She was out in a flash.

He moved as fast as he had ever moved in his life, and caught up with her before she could run. He slid an arm round her waist, as if to hug her, and people looking on could have what ideas they liked.

"What's all this?" he demanded sharply.

"Let me go, or I'll scream!"

"Scream and I'll call the police," Rollison said with great deliberation; "I'll tell them about Dutch Himmy and Wilf, and everything that goes with it."

Until that moment, Valerie was taut and struggling in his grip; suddenly, she stopped, and went almost limp. She turned to look at him. The fire in her eyes made her almost beautiful.

"You beast, I believe you would," she said.

"And how right you are."

"You'd get Wilf killed!"

"You're going the right way about doing that yourself. Let's get back into the car and talk this out."

"I'm not going to that farm."

"Why not?"

"I want to stay in New York. I might hear from Brian Conway at any time; he knows I'm there."

"How do you know that?" Rollison inquired mildly.

"He telephoned me," Valerie said; "he told me Dutch - Dutch Himmy had heard you'd been to see that man Day, and he had the Belle Hotel watched. And I don't care what you say, when I know where to take the jewels, I'll take them. Then Wilf will be all right."

"If Brian ever gives you that kind of message from Dutch Himmy, he'll be lying," Rollison said, quietly.

"You only say that," Valerie accused him, wildly; "you haven't liked Brian Conway from the beginning. How do I know that he's a fraud? I've only your word for it."

"That's right," said Rollison, sorrowfully; "you've only my word and your own wits for that and a lot of other things - including this: if you don't come to the farm and if you don't stay there without giving trouble, I'll telephone the whole story of Wilf's kidnapping to the police and the press."

He wouldn't do that of course; but would Valerie call his bluff?

He waited, feeling almost as sad as he had sounded, but realising that he had been wrong to take her acquiescence for granted; he had reckoned without the mind that Valerie could truly call her own. Now, she had to agree or compel him to use a form of violence he hadn't anticipated and didn't like.

"If anything happens to Wilf, I shall always blame you," she said, bitterly, and shrugged herself free and went back to the car. A moment later, they were sitting side by side.

"Val," Rollison said, "there's a lot of evidence that Al Cadey wasn't really working for Dutch Himmy, but that he was cashing in because he knew that Wilf had been kidnapped.

There's more evidence that you don't yet know what terms Dutch Himmy will demand for Wilf's release. I've checked as closely as I can, and come to the conclusion that you aren't safe in New York, that the wise thing is to get you out. I'll find out what terms Dutch Himmy will offer, and then we can talk business. Why not see it my way?" When she didn't answer, he went on: "You know, Wilf did give me a job."

"Oh, I know!" said Valerie, and surprisingly melted suddenly and pressed his hand. It was a remarkable volte face, and almost suspicious. "Don't think I'm ungrateful, Rolly, but I just don't believe a word you say. You're simply trying to look after me. Well, I don't care about me; I'm only worried about Wilf."

"My word on it," Rollison said, "I think this is the best way to find out what Dutch Himmy will take in exchange for Wilf. Before we come to any terms, we have to be sure that Wilf's still all right, don't we?" That hurt her, and he let it sink in. "He probably is, but we can't be sure."

"I suppose not," agreed Valerie, in a muffled voice. "All right, Rolly. I'm sorry I tried to run off, but" - she gave a smile that was almost radiant - "I knew it wouldn't be any good arguing with you."

He chuckled.

They laughed.

He studied the map and, a little further on at a garage where hundreds of used cars were on sale, he left the Cadillac for some work to be done on imaginary pump trouble, and drove off again in a sky-blue Pontiac. When he reached the little village of Ridgway, where Mellish was to meet him, he felt quite sure they had not been followed.

It was fifteen minutes' drive to the farm, off the main road. The countryside looked rich and fertile. There were fruit-orchards. There were cattle and, at the farm, fowl and pigs. Tim Mellish was a matured forty-five, and his wife Mary an evergreen forty, with a natural native friendliness which made the world feel at ease. Within ten minutes, Valerie had settled down as if she was one of the family.

Outside, Mellish said soberly:

"How serious is it, Rolly?" When Rollison didn't answer, he added: "You sure you were right when you mentioned Dutch Himmy?"

"Yes."

"Then it couldn't be much more serious," Tim said. "I'd better be blunt."

"Please," said Rollison.

"If trouble looks like developing, I shall have to call in the police."

"Don't wait too long," Rollison pleaded; "don't take any chances, Tim. But with luck these johnnies haven't the faintest idea where Valerie is. I covered my traces, and"

"I'm not expecting trouble, but I had to warn you," Mellish said. "And you - be careful. Dutch Himmy isn't going to take a slap in the face lying down."

Thus it was made obvious that even this homely family on their remote little farm knew and feared Dutch Himmy.

The Toff drove cheerfully and almost gaily back to the garage where he had left the Cadillac, and paid a bill for work which had not been necessary; a modest bill, though, where he could easily have been fleeced. In the Cadillac, he drove less gaily, for he believed it possible that the car would be picked out among the hundreds which were going his way.

He studied the map again and, striking north, avoided Holland Tunnel and went over the Washington Bridge. By then, the first bright lights were showing in the fairyland of New York, the first touch of magic was in the evening air. Now, traffic was mostly coming out of town, not in. At the far end, he turned into Broadway, deciding to give the Parkway a miss, and he hadn't driven more than two hundred yards before a car swung across his bows.

He could swing the wheel, tear the bumpers and get away, or he could take what was coming. In broad daylight and with a hundred cars and several policemen in sight, he did not greatly fear.

Tall, ungainly Legs, whose real name was Leggatt, uncoiled himself from the Mercury and, grinning, came towards him.

"Been places?" he asked.

"Just sight-seeing," said Rollison. "How's Cy?"

"Cy's fine. He wants to see you alive tomorrow."

"May he live not to regret it."

"Seriously, pal," Legs said, and pushed his head further into the car. He had a leathery face with a droll expression, and rather narrow blue eyes. "You're in trouble."

"With you or Cy?"

"Dutch Himmy has put a curtain call out for you."

Rollison didn't speak.

"We picked up the call," explained Legs. "It goes this way. Everything was working smoothly until you came along. True, there was some trouble with Cadey, who was striking out on his own - the way I've heard the story, Conway realised Cadey wasn't playing the game in the right way, but Conway's big mistake was letting you follow him. Conway's a Dutch Himmy man, and he's been told to do his next job better - or else."

"Dutch a pal of yours?" asked Rollison, mildly.

Legs grinned.

"Cy Day's got his spies, even in Dutch's parlour. And Dutch made a point of passing word to Cy, so that Cy could tell you. Or" Legs stopped smiling just for a moment. "Or warn you. Dutch doesn't care about Cadey, who was double-crossing him."

"Legs," interrupted Rollison, "how many of Cy's agents were out looking for me?"

"Two at every tunnel and every bridge and every approach to them all," Legs told him, flatly. "Cy just wants to save you from being hurt. He says that if you care to stay as his guest at the Belle Hotel, you'll be all right. You'd better tell him where you took Valerie, because if she's found by Dutch Himmy" Legs broke off.

"Legs," Rollison said again more quietly, "tell Cy I'll never be able to thank him enough, but I'm going to play this my way. I think he over-rates Dutch Himmy and at the same time he under-rates himself. We'll see."

Legs put his head on one side.

"Which do you prefer?" he asked. "Lilies or roses?"

"Please yourself," said Rollison.

"Okay. While you're getting ready to die," Legs went on, "keep this in mind, will you? Cy would like to see you, to tell you who Mark Quentin is."

Legs grinned, and turned away.

But it was a night, the Toff decided, when Cy Day would have to wait.

Now, it was as dark as mid-town New York ever allowed night to be. It was noisy, too. In his suite at the Arden-Astoria, Rollison looked out of the window and saw the traffic and, in the distance, saw the glow of light in the sky. It was then a little after eight o'clock.

There had been no messages.

There had been no trouble.

There had been waiting, watching men.

He went out, and when he reached Park Avenue, he saw the faithful Sikoski at the wheel of his cab, intent on the comic art. The cabby looked up with a start and repeated the performance of folding the book and sliding it into his pocket.

"Okay," he said.

"If you were me," said Rollison, "where would you eat?"

Sikoski grinned. "You mean eat? Or look?"

"Can you manage both?"

The cabby put his head back, and grinned happily.

"Colonel," he said, "you and me will always get along. Sure, there's a place down in the Village where you can eat good and see plenty." He started off, and when they were a few blocks nearer Greenwich Village, he leaned back and asked nonchalantly: "You want to know something?"

"We're being followed."

"Colonel," breathed Sikoski, "the more I see you the more I like you. Do you want trouble tonight, or do you want to dodge it? I can give it you both ways."

"As it comes."

"Fine," said Sikoski. "Just fine. Don't say I didn't warn you to hold on."

He drove like a firecracker out of control. He weaved, looped and sometimes seemed to fly through and over the traffic. He took corners on two wheels and he sent Rollison, breathless and even scared, heavily against one door or the other. In twenty minutes he beat a dozen lights; and in twenty minutes he was slowing down in a narrow street in the only New York section with narrow streets which criss-crossed one another without plan. He wiped his forehead as he did this, and said:

"You want to know something?"

"Bud," said Rollison, "we're being followed."

"You never said a truer word, Colonel. You still want to eat?"

"Yes. And Bud . . ."

"Yeh?"

"If you telephone Cy Day, I won't be all that grateful. There are some games that have to be played a different way."

"Okay, Colonel," Sikoski said. "I'm your man."

Five minutes later, Rollison went into a night-club called Sapelli's. From the outside, it was nothing but a doorway with a few photographs of a tease artist and a coloured singer. Down narrow stairs and along a narrow passage, was a small bar; beyond it, a circular-shaped room with tables round the sides, a space for dancing. Every table was placed so that every diner had a good view of the floor. No one was dancing, but a pianist, out of sight, was playing Viennese music. Two waiters took Rollison to his table, a blonde and a brunette at the bar looked his way but didn't rush him.

A man followed, almost on his heels, and came towards him. He was small and dark and swarthy. He carried a newspaper under his arm, and it wouldn't have surprised anyone if he carried a gun there, too. His eyes were narrowed; flinty. He walked very slowly and deliberately, and managed to make most of the diners and most of the people at the bar look edgy. One couple left the bar and went out.

The man paused in front of Rollison's table. A waiter, approaching, turned tail and hurried through the service door. In flight?

Rollison looked up into the swarthy face.

"Good evening," he said, amiably.

The man took the newspaper from under his arm and dropped it on to the Toff's table. Then he turned and went to another table, opposite; from there he could watch everything Rollison did.

Rollison sensed the easing of tension and marvelled at the way it had come into the room. The pianist swung into lively, modern stuff. Two couples began to dance. Most of the diners glanced at Rollison, covertly; few took any notice of the swarthy man.

Rollison opened the newspaper....

As the Toff, he had made the front page. So had two other stories - the death of Al Cadey and the finding of a body in a laundry basket which had been taken from the Arden-Astoria. There were photographs, of the basket and the body, and there was a description of the man and his name: Mark Quentin, partner in the accountancy company of Quentin, Tenby and Russell, Incorporated.

Van Russell's partner had died in Valerie's arms; and Cy Day had wanted Rollison to know.

Rollison looked up into the eyes of the swarthy man, who stared back without blinking. The waiter found his courage and brought half-a-dozen blue points with some brown bread and butter. Rollison ate, and then looked through the rest of the newspaper, from the sport to the society pages, and saw nothing else that really interested him. He folded it, when a grilled sole arrived. Delicious. He was through a steak so superbly cooked in a sauce which must have been conceived in Paris when the lights began to dim. He glanced across at the swarthy man, who had taken something from his pocket and laid it on the table, under a table napkin.

A gun.

Then, the girl came on.

At first glimpse, she was nice. Not very tall, but obviously with everything. Modest, though. She wore an ordinary three-quarter-length dress, black and silver; the silver part of it shimmered. She had long fair hair, brushed sleekly to her shoulders, nice arms and legs. The spotlight was on her. She began to dance, and as she danced there was a voluptuous rhythm in the music, and in her body; an unbelievable change. Her hands seemed everywhere; she was Eve, she was Adam and Eve, she was boy and girl, she was Sodom and Gomorrah. Her dress shimmered as she writhed, and she slid out of it gradually as a snake would slide out of its skin, and she went on and on stripping, in the light that was hardly light at all.

Throughout this, the swarthy man watched Rollison with the intentness of a snake.

The dancer drew nearer Rollison, writhing, the light just sufficient to glow on her fine, firm young body. She stroked the cheek of a man near Rollison, patted another's head, kissed another lightly, and seemed to be inviting them to hurl themselves at her. She came towards Rollison, and her smile was the smile of Delilah; she leaned over him and put her hands on either side of his face, then slowly and deliberately kissed him - and as she withdrew her lips, she said:

"There's a drunk at the bar; watch him, too. I'm with Cy Day."

She drew away.

She went to a man two tables removed, and the man began to sweat. Women sat, as if fascinated. Then, the lights flashed on and the dancer shrieked and ran, as if taken completely by surprise, while the swarthy man looked at Rollison with that snake-like intensity, and a big, powerful man at the bar began to talk too loudly, as if he was rolling drunk.

There was dancing.

Rollison called a waiter.

"The original blonde at the bar," Rollison said, "would she care to dance?"

"I'll ask her for you," the waiter said.

The music was slow, sensuous, of the jungle; exactly the right music for the moment. The blonde and the brunette wouldn't lack custom, now; and suddenly there were several more of them; replicas. The waiter approached the one whom Rollison had pointed out, and she looked across and smiled. Ten years ago, she would have been rather easy on the eye. She came across and sat down, and Rollison ordered champagne.

"I'm not sure I'm going to be safe with you," the girl said, "and I don't mean that the way my mother would. I'm Anita . . ."

"Thanks. I'm . . ."

"I can read the newspaper, too, Toff," she said. "You want some advice from me?"

"Go back where I came from?"

She laughed. "All right, let's dance," she said; "nothing will happen here."

Rollison stood up, and they danced. She was very light on her feet, and he knew that she was one of the women who liked dancing for its own sake, not for the cheek-to-cheek and the pinching and the squeezing; once, she had been a really nice girl. They finished the dance, sat one out, emptied the bottle and ordered another, and started to dance again. The drunk at the bar got drunker, and no one interfered; the snake at the table sat as still as a man could, while eating and drinking and smoking. Rollison took the blonde in his arms and began to hold her tight, and she thrust her head back and said:

"So they're all alike."

"Under the cloth on my table there's a hundred-dollar bill," Rollison whispered; "all for you." He hugged her until she couldn't be any closer, and he kissed her cheek and her ears - and when he was level with the swarthy man, he thrust her bodily into the table and the man. In the same movement, he grabbed a bottle and sprang across the dance-floor. He saw the drunk stop drooling, and saw his hand flash to his pocket, but it didn't flash fast enough. Rollison flung the bottle and caught him on the cheek, and then turned for the door by the side of the bar, for the passage, the staircase and, he prayed, Sikoski.

15

COURTESY CALL

SIKOSKI was there.

It looked as if he had been waiting for trouble from the moment Rollison had disappeared, because the moment Rollison reached the car, the engine was turning. They were round the first corner before anyone else appeared from the club, and they were not followed. Sikoski took no chances this time, but hurtled towards the East River Parkway and then north, until even he must be sure that no danger threatened.

He turned off, at 72nd Street.

"New York exciting enough for you today?" he inquired, smugly.

"It's doing fine, pardner, real fine," boomed Rollison, and they grinned. "If there's any life in this old dogie, take me to the Mil west Hotel, will you?"

"Sure, Colonel, sure."

The" journey took twenty minutes. Traffic was not thick, but they had bad luck with lights. Rollison lit a cigarette, and smoothed down his hair, and pondered deeply. There were even more good reasons for thinking that Cy Day knew New York better than he did.

They were forced to stop by a news-stand, and he wound down his window.

"Night Telegram" he called; Dando's tabloid was more likely

to give him what he wanted to read about than one of the other papers. The exchange of thick newspaper and a quarter was swift and easy, and the cab moved off. Rollison looked through the headlines, finding the light quite bright enough. He found what he wanted on the back page, guessed that earlier stories had been pushed off, and that in the next editions it would have most of the front page.

MILLIONAIRE PLAYGIRL KIDNAPPED
VALERIE HALL, PART OWNER ATYEO BUILDING
Mystery of Black Cadillac

There wasn't really much beyond the headlines. No one had connected the Toff with the kidnapping story, although he was on the same page. So was the death of Russell's partner, and that sobered Rollison. He tore off the outer pages, and left the rest on the seat, and sat back for five minutes. Then, they slid to a standstill outside the Milwest Hotel, which was near Central Park, and Sikoski screwed his thick neck round and said with a rush:

"You-want-to-know-something-we-ain't-bin-followed."

"If you go on like this," Rollison said, "you'll soon be buying yourself a new cab. One that will go fast." He got out, knowing that he didn't need to tell Sikoski where to go; Sikoski would be at hand if there were another emergency. So far, no one had followed him. He didn't ask at the desk for Brian Conway, for he had Conway's room number. There was a sleepy coloured bell-cum-elevator boy who gave him a lazy, attractive smile and a husky: "You're welcome." At the seventh floor Rollison stepped into the passage. He didn't go straight to Conway's room, for it was possible that he had been followed from the hall; two men had been sitting there. He gave them five minutes, and when no one arrived, decided that they weren't watching for him, or keeping a watch on Conway or Halloran. He went along to Conway's room, but didn't tap; he examined the lock, and realised that it wouldn't be easy, like that at Cadey's apartment; but it could be done.

It took him four minutes.

The lock clicked back, and it was possible that anyone inside the room had heard it. There was no sound. Rollison opened the door, on to darkness. He stepped inside swiftly, and flattened himself against the wall; if he had been heard, then Conway might be standing there, gun poised.

There was still no sound.

Rollison switched on a light.

This was a one-room apartment, reached through a little cubicle with three doors - one, behind him, one into a shower and toilet, one into the bedroom. He went in. There was a big bed, a chest and a wardrobe. Conway's clothes were still here, nothing suggested that the man had gone. Rollison ran through all he could find, and discovered nothing of interest, not even telephone numbers. He went next door, and repeated the whole performance, taking less time with the lock.

Halloran was still in residence, too.

Rollison found nothing helpful in that room, and went back to Conway's. He fixed the door, so that it did not show that it had been forced, and stretched out on the bed, smoking, looking at the ceiling, and waiting for the slightest sound. He told himself that it would be worth waiting for an hour, but in two minutes he was up again. Without closing the door properly, he went downstairs to a telephone call-box from which he could see the front door - and anyone who came in. He lifted the telephone, and called Tim Mellish.

The call came through with the familiar bewildering speed.

"Yes, Rolly, everything's fine," greeted Mary Mellish; "you don't need to worry. I've been telling Tim that. And Valerie's a very lovely girl; we're getting along just like old friends. Right now, we're playing canasta, but we're going to watch television soon so don't call up any more, will you?"

"No, ma'am," said Rollison, humbly. "Good night."

He went back to Conway's room, which was still empty.

It was good to know that nothing had misfired with Valerie; he told himself that he could be quite sure that it wouldn't, now, because he hadn't been traced. But he was edgy. He called

Cy Day's home, but there was no answer. He called the Belle Hotel and asked for Legs, and Legs answered very soon.

"Legs, did your men send in any report to say where I'd been?" Rollison asked.

Legs said: "Nope."

"None at all?"

"Nope."

"Thanks."

"Sweet-smelling flowers," Legs said.

Rollison was smiling when he rang off. He lit a cigarette, and was glad to relax.

He could be sure that he had made Dutch Himmy very mad by now; and if Dando knew his stuff, then Dutch Himmy would already be suspecting that rival gang. It ought to be worth buying every newspaper in New York tomorrow.

Then, he heard footsteps in the passage.

He swung his legs off the bed, and moved swiftly towards the wall, alongside the bathroom. A key sounded in the lock, and immediately afterwards, Mike Halloran said in that unforgettable voice:

"Sure, get some sleep, Brian."

Another door opened.

Brian Conway came in, closed the door, put the chain into position instead, and then came into the room. By that time, there was no sound of Halloran. Rollison saw Conway's dejected shoulders, the droop of his mouth. Without glancing sideways, Conway went across to the bed, taking off his bow tie as he did so. Then, he turned round.

He nearly crumpled up when he saw Rollison, and might have fallen but for the bed. He grabbed it, to steady himself. His mouth dropped open and his eyes shimmered with fear. He tried to speak but made only a gibberish of sound.

"Hi, Brian," said Rollison, pleasantly; "someone been giving you evil thoughts?"

"Wh - wh - what are you doing here?"

"I really wanted to inquire after your health," said Rollison, sweetly, "and after your friends, of course. Especially Al Cadey."

Brian Conway was at the old game; trembling violently.

"I - I don't know who you mean!"

"You mean to say you shot a stranger?" exclaimed the Toff, horrified. "My Brian, why? That's far worse; a little gun-play between friends may be forgiven, but a stranger - why, poor, poor Al."

Conway didn't even try to speak.

"I needn't tell anyone in person," said Rollison, earnestly. "I could just breathe a word to Dando of the Night Telegram, to look for your prints at Al's place. He'd publish it with pleasure, and then where would you be?"

"Rollison, I - I thought he'd kill Val Hall; I swear I did. I knew he was as bad as they come, and - and I couldn't risk it. I'd like to keep her safe; if I could get away from Dutch I would; why - why I named him. Didn't I? I told Val and I told you he was behind it, didn't I? I hoped you'd get Dutch."

He broke off.

"I bet you hoped," said Rollison, softly. "Why don't you come across, and admit that you like working for Dutch Himmy? You were planted to travel with Valerie, and to take her straight to Al."

"That wasn't the way of it," Conway muttered. "I had to get those jewels, that was my job, but she insisted on coming along. I "

He broke off.

Rollison glanced away from him, towards the door, and he felt something of Conway's flare of alarm. There was a sharp tap; then another, before there was any chance to answer. Conway looked imploringly at Rollison.

"See who it is," whispered Rollison, and crept into the bathroom.

Conway moved slowly towards the door, and braced himself. When he called out, his voice was commendably steady.

"Who wants me?"

"Is that Brian Conway?"

"I asked who wants me?"

"I want to talk to you."

"Who are you?"

"Just open up," the man said, "or I'll break the door down and break you with it."

It wasn't a powerful voice, but high-pitched and intense. It was familiar, too, in the way that Dando's had been. Conway gulped, and still looked at Rollison, who whispered:

"Handle it your way."

Conway took a gun from his pocket. He was quick with a gun, and the fact that he had killed the night before hadn't made him get rid of this one; Rollison wondered if it was the same automatic.

"Wait a minute," Conway called to the man outside.

He stood to one side, unfastened the chain noisily, so that whoever was in the passage could hear it, and then let it fall. It rattled. Gun poised, he stood to one side. The door was thrust open, but no one came in at once, for there was a sharp call out there:

"Hold it!"

Only Halloran had a voice so much like a closing steel trap.

Rollison was just able to see into the passage. He ought to have recognised the first voice as readily as he had recognised the face before. The man who had come ready to break the door down was Van Russell. His head was still bandaged, and he had a patch over his closed eye. He stood looking round at Halloran, who had heard the shouting and had come to Conway's rescue.

"You want to see Brian," said Halloran; "so go on, see Brian." He was out of sight; but his voice and manner suggested that he was carrying a gun.

Conway had the sense not to call out.

Russell came in, sideways. Halloran followed, and as he

entered, Rollison dropped his hand to the other's wrist, wrenched, and took the gun away. It was as quick and easy as that. Halloran gave a grinding croak of protest, that was all. Conway didn't even try to put up a fight, just held his gun towards the floor, and waited until Rollison ordered:

"Mike, close the door."

Halloran closed it, with his foot

Russell said: "What is this?"

"That's what I'd like to know from you," Rollison said, chidingly. "I'm quite sure your sister Julie doesn't know you're out. What brought you to Conway?"

Russell said, in a very hard voice:

"In one way, you did. You told me about him and Halloran. Then I discovered that a friend of mine had been murdered. A partner and a friend of mine. I'll get this killer, if—" He broke off, as if too keyed up to finish; there was a film of tears in his eye.

Rollison said mildly: "What made you think that Brian Conway might know anything about it?"

"I didn't have any other contact with Dutch Himmy."

"But I don't know Dutch Himmy," cried Conway. "Sure, I've done some jobs for him, but I don't know him!"

"How about your friend?" Rollison asked, softly.

"Me?" clanked Halloran. "No, sir; I did a stretch once for Al Cadey, who was a leg-man of Dutch Himmy. Why did I do it? I spent five years inside for a job I didn't do, Mr. Toff, because Dutch Himmy said he would put a finger on me if I didn't. Don't ask me anything about Dutch Himmy, I wouldn't know a thing if I knew everything."

Russell went slowly towards the bed, and dropped on to it. He looked all in. It was easy to imagine that his rage had given him a false strength, that the desire for revenge had brought him here, raging; but now that he realised he had wasted his time, it was too much for him.

"Now let's find out if this is true," Rollison said.

Half an hour later, he wasn't absolutely sure that it was true.

He was sure that he wouldn't get any more out of Conway or Halloran.

Rollison gave Russell a helping hand into the lift; and a few seconds later, a hand out of it. Russell limped badly, but didn't say why; there seemed to be something the matter with his waist. This was a quiet street. A few cars were parked with drivers in them; otherwise no one else was about. Sikoski sat in his inevitable way, poring over a comic strip book; or else he was dozing, Rollison couldn't be sure which. He was fifty yards away, a good enough position - and obviously he wasn't expecting trouble.

Rollison would have been, but for his preoccupation with Russell.

"If I take you home," he said, "can I be sure you'll stay there? Or would it be better if . . ."

"Just drive me back home," Russell said, in a lifeless voice. "I'm all washed up, and I know it. Wilf Hall and Mark Quentin, the two of them." There was something like a sob in his voice. "Just take me home, will you, and then"

That was the moment when Rollison first felt sharply suspicious; of Sikoski; or rather, of the man sitting where Sikoski should be. The head was still bowed. The skullcap was still tight. But there was no ring of dark curly hair beneath it. Sikoski wasn't in the cab; someone else was.

It was the only cab in sight; a red-and-yellow one.

"Russell," Rollison said, very softly, "I'm in a jam. I'm going to have to run for it. I'll edge you towards a doorway, and you stay there; you'll be out of the way if there's any shooting."

Russell straightened up. "What . . ." he began.

That was all.

There was no time for Rollison to run. The driver who wasn't Sikoski straightened up, three men stepped like marionettes from dark doorways, and he was covered by three guns. If they'd come to kill, this was it.

16

FLOOR 101

NONE of them fired.

Rollison sensed that they would if he ran; wasn't sure that it would serve any purpose if he let them take him. He hadn't much time to think. If they had set out to kill, would there be any point in taking him away first? They could shoot and leave him here.

Couldn't they?

One man said: "Okay, Toff, get in." He moved swiftly, gripped Russell's arm, and sent him staggering away from the cab. "Just get in, with your pal," the man ordered Rollison.

'Pal' meant Sikoski.

Another man opened the door.

There were people on the other side of the street, and there were the double-parked cars; none of the people in sight could have guessed what was happening. Rollison had lost any chance he ever had. He got in, and nearly stumbled over Sikoski's body.

Body?

A man pushed him, and climbed in after him. He was thrust into a corner. The fake cabby took the wheel and they started off - with a private car in front, the taxi next, another private car behind; this explained the double parking. The lights of New York slid by them, but Rollison didn't see many of them;

he didn't see the first movement either, but felt the smashing blow on the nape of his neck.

He went out.

When he came round, there were subdued lights. He was on his feet, and being dragged along; his legs were actually working a little, so the reflexes were in good order. One man was on one side of him, another on the other.

He was too dazed to think beyond what he just glimpsed; he did not even remember how this had happened. But as his head cleared and he began to think back, they reached the doors of an elevator.

One was open.

Rollison looked right and left. He saw empty passages on either side, and unlit glass windows. It was like a street within a building but without open sky above. As he was pushed into the elevator he realised what it was: the concourse of one of the skyscrapers of the city.

Which one?

Did it matter?

He leaned against the glossy wooden sides. The doors closed. The elevator gave a little whining sound, and they started to go up. Head still whirling, Rollison saw the indicator built in one side - the floor indicator.

10 - 20 - 30 - 40....

There were 90. Ninety. The lights flashed as they passed each tenth floor. He knew enough of the tall buildings to realise that this was an express lift, missing all but every tenth floor.

They slid to a standstill, and the doors opened automatically. He was half pushed and half dragged out, but the journey wasn't yet at an end; just along the passage was another elevator, and the sign sticking out from it said: Local. Floors 90 to 101.

They went in.

This elevator was much slower, and the journey seemed to take as long as the first. Rollison couldn't be sure whether it did or not. His head was screaming, and when they pushed him out, he almost fell. They saved him. He was aware of lights in the distance, and darkness close by. Lights and darkness, shadowy figures, white stars above and a rainbow of stars below. He leaned against the wall and took in deep, shivering breaths, hoping that it would help to clear his head. It did. They left him alone, now. He straightened up, and saw that there were several figures, just the heads and shoulders of men against the strange distant light. Stars above and stars below. He moved slowly towards one of the shadowy figures, which moved to one side, to let him pass. He realised that he had come up against a wall of glass; it was glass from about the height of his waist upwards, anyhow. With his nose against the glass he looked out and saw the street lights below, something like the view from an aircraft. Red, blue, yellow and green, lights everywhere, pools of light, lanes of light, and great patches of darkness.

He looked up, and saw the same silent stars above him; either there was no roof just there, or it was of glass.

In a way, the worst of all this was the silence. No one spoke. There were the lights below, a hundred and one floors below, and the stars above. Rollison looked right and left. Two buildings, one with a red star and the other with a blue light, seemed about on a level with this one; others, with yellow lights still at their windows, were much lower than the spot where he stood. One hundred and one floors...

The Atyeo Building had exactly that number.

Rollison looked round again. The shadowy figures stood still and silent. Why didn't they speak? They were trying to break his nerve, of course; but it would take a lot of this to succeed. If only he could sit down. If only there was some light. If only they would speak.

He couldn't stand here any longer.

He began to move towards the right, and almost prayed that someone would call out, to stop him, but no one said a thing and no one moved. Outlined against the windows were the heads and shoulders, like dummies, standing there to watch him and to make sure that he knew that he wasn't alone. The silence seemed to scream at him. There was no sound from the streets, from the countless moving lights - and none from the green and red lights of aircraft which moved across the sky.

Rollison saw a light over a doorway, which said: Elevator. He passed it. No one followed him; it was as if they knew that he couldn't get away, and that there was nothing to worry about if he tried. He walked slowly. There was a waist-high wall, and windows above it, and he saw the whole of New York spread out beneath him. He came again, in the semi-darkness, to the sign marked Elevator, and knew that he had walked right round the top of the Atyeo Building. What did they call it? The Observation Tower - and only one in New York was higher.

He went to a window again and looked out, and still no one spoke.

Why didn't they speak?

Were they men? Or dummies? Was this some hideous dream? He remembered being struck over the head, he could conceivably be having illusions.

He approached the nearest man, and opened his mouth - and then closed it again. Once he spoke, it would break the spell, and that was what they wanted; to unnerve him. Let them try! He put his hands to his pockets for a cigarette; his packet wasn't where he usually kept it. He tried the next pocket; it wasn't there, either. In something like a panic, he tried again and again, feeling in pockets where he never kept cigarettes; and there was none.

He had his lighter.

He let it drop back into the pocket, and started another walk, clenching his teeth this time but determined not to let them break his nerve. He drew level with one of the silhouettes, passed - and kicked against an outstretched leg. He went sprawling, and banged an elbow and his chin. He lay on the floor for a few seconds, glaring round in the darkness. Then, he picked himself up, savagely. His arms were rigid by his sides as he walked on, taking every step very carefully. He heard no sound - except one that was coming to his ears clearly now, the sound of men breathing. There was nothing really odd about it, and yet it had an eeriness which began to play on his nerves. It was as if they were all breathing in at the same time, and letting their breath out at the same time, too; softly and hissingly. He found himself thinking about that so much that he kicked against another outstretched leg, without remembering that one might be there.

This time, he banged his forehead painfully.

He took longer to get up, and when he did stand again, he peered about him. His own breathing was now so hard that it drowned the sound of the other; he couldn't hear it at all. Yet he could see the heads and the shoulders and felt that he wanted to rush at one of them and strike the man, beat at his face, try to break his neck.

That was what they wanted.

He must keep his nerve.

He started off again, walking very slowly, and made two complete circuits of the observation tower; nothing happened. Then, he heard a different sound; a rustling. He sprang round towards it, and something struck his face, and burst. In that first moment, he was aware only of anger; and then something bit at his eyes and his lips and his nose, and the pain was so great that he wanted to scream; but he would not. He staggered back, and for a while they let him put his hands to his eyes, let him gasp and fight for breath, until at last he felt easier. The last of the stinging eased.

Clenching his teeth, he started off again.

This time, he hadn't gone ten feet before they struck at him - and now they were in earnest. They used sticks, whips, fists, and feet. He whirled and struck out, but it was useless; he could not save himself. He covered his face with his hands and crouched, trying desperately to keep away from the worst of the blows. He remembered two men kicking Van Russell. . . .

Here, there were no lights; no one to shout for the police; no help at all.

As suddenly as the assault began, it stopped.

A man said: "Rollison, I want you to answer a few questions."

17
QUESTIONS

THE Toff heard, but did not answer.

He was dazed and badly bruised, and there was a sharp pain in his left shoulder, but he heard the question, which came slowly into the quiet after the assault. Yet the blood pounded in his ears, and it was as if a great wind was blowing outside this mighty tower.

If they started again ...

He wanted time; time, to recover; time, to stiffen his resolve; time, to think. If they started again, he would find it hard not to surrender completely, but ... "Rollison," the man said again, "I want to ask you a few questions."

The Toff didn't answer.

A minute would help; three or four minutes would be invaluable. He felt more on top of himself even now. This man wanted to ask questions, and that was like a shining light into the future - for he wouldn't kill until he'd had his answers.

Would he?

The voice was hard, but not metallic like Halloran's. It had the edge of cruelty, too. The Toff had an impression that it came from the corner of the man's lips, that the speaker didn't open his mouth properly; but that could be no more than an impression, for it was still dark.

"I can wake him up," another man said.

The first speaker answered quickly.

"See if he's okay."

A light went on, and Rollison sensed it, although it could not fall on his eyes. He lay almost at full length, with one knee bent. They had turned him on his back, his face towards the ground, his body limp. Was it torchlight? It grew brighter, and he knew that it was a torch which might strike his eyes at any moment. Then, a man knelt down, took his right shoulder and pulled him round. The light stabbed into his closed eyes, but he had the second's warning that he needed, and he kept his eyelids still.

A hand groped and found his pulse.

"He's alive," said that man who had offered to wake him.

The voice seemed to get further away as the man stood up; the light was diffused. Rollison's head still ached but he was less dizzy, and now he wouldn't be such easy game. He let himself fall back limply, in spite of the pain at his shoulder. There were whispers, movements, metallic sounds, and he tried to guess what they were doing. The vital thing at the moment was that they wanted him alive because of those questions, but - what would they do to try to make him answer?

Footsteps.

There was a splashing sound, and then water struck him in the face, powerfully enough to hurt. He winced, and turned his head, and his eyes nickered. The water ran into his eyes, his nostrils and his mouth, soaking his shirt and collar. He didn't 'come round' at once, but lay there as a man said:

"He's awake."

"Sit him up," said the man with the hard voice.

Now, two of them took his shoulders, and the pain at the left shoulder was very bad; he grunted with it. They dragged him to his feet and then towards one side of the promenade, and dumped him into a chair. It was a relief to sit. His head was much clearer, but he let his chin fall to his chest, as if he was still semi-conscious; he must look like a drowned rat.

"Shall I give him some more?" the man asked.

"Yes."

Well, cold water was refreshing, wasn't it? Once the shock was over, Rollison told himself that he would feel better, and that he would have gained more time. If he had needed telling how badly this man wanted the answers to his questions, this was it. He braced himself. This time, the water was held above his head and poured out in a steady stream; he clenched his teeth against the first impact, and then tried to raise his head and flickered his eyes, as if he was really coming round.

Water dripped off him; everywhere.

He blinked about him, able to see much more than he pretended. There was a dim light, not good enough to show very much, but he could make out the figures of a group of men, one of them a little apart from the others. He wore a wide-brimmed hat pulled low over his eyes, a raincoat which seemed out of place, for it was warm; and a mask. The mask didn't pretend to be anything else; it was just a child's plaything, shiny red and pink; there was even a painted moustache. It covered every part of the stranger's face; and that might be to make sure that the men didn't see him - not simply to make sure that the Toff had no chance to identify him.

"Rollison," he said, "who brought you over here?"

That question Rollison could answer, but not yet. He could gain more time. He was feeling very much better, even felt that he had control of his arms and legs; the pain at his shoulder was slightly easier, too. He raised his head and peered at the man as if his eyes were hurting him, and he licked his wet lips.

"Wha - what?" he croaked.

"Who brought you over here?"

"You - you did," said Rollison, as if foolishly. "Men attack - men attacked me."

"And you know what it will be like if they attack you again," the man said. His voice was still hard, slow and measured; an assumed voice, of course, he meant to make sure that no single feature was identifiable. "I don't mean who brought you up to the top of the building, I mean who brought you to New York."

Rollison gulped, and looked dull and stupid.

"Who brou' - oh, now I un'erstand!" He paused, to breathe very heavily, as if it was an effort to talk. Time. He was even beginning to wonder what would happen if he made a dive for the elevator. He could see it, with the doors standing open; there was a pale white light inside. Closer to him, the light seemed dimmer, now, and was an unflattering greeny-blue. It was possible to see the stars and in the distance the lights of the environs of New York. "Wilf - Wilfred Hall," he added.

The man said: "Okay, I know that's true. Did Hall name anyone he was nervous about?"

So that was it; they wanted to know how much Rollison knew. He might have a chance to stall, to keep them in a state of uncertainty, but if they believed he could answer and name one of them, they would be merciless.

At first play foolish; dazed.

"It was Wilf Hall," he muttered. "Sent me a cable, then - wrote to me." He paused and gasped again. They stood round him, apparently unimpressed, all full of menace. "Asked me to look - to look after Valerie." He opened his eyes wide and stared straight into the slits of the mask. "Wilf's sister."

"I know who Valerie is," the man said. "Did he name anyone?"

"Eh?"

The man kept patient. "Let's get it straight. When did Hall write to you?"

" 'Bout a week - 'bout a week ago," Rollison answered, and his hand moved towards his pocket. "I've

He snatched his hand away.

Two of the shadowy figures, moved so swiftly that he flinched; one grabbed one arm, the other stood over him with an automatic.

Rollison flung his left arm up, trying to shake the man's grip, and for the first time since he had come round his voice held a note of shrill defiance.

"What's the matter with them? I'm only going to show you the letter!"

"Do you have it with you?" The man sounded eager.

"Should - should be in my pocket."

"Okay," the man said, "get it, but don't try any tricks with palm guns or any of the little gadgets you're fond of at home."

Rollison found a slow grin; as if that pleased him.

He could show the letter, which named no one, and that couldn't do anything but good.

"You been reading about me?" he asked, and slid his hands towards his pocket again. He sensed the tension of the other men, and heard one breathe:

"Dutch, you don't want to take any chances."

Dutch.

Rollison didn't stop what he was doing, even at the sound of the name. He took out his wallet, and the thin airmail letter was folded inside. He started to unfold it, but Dutch Himmy stepped forward and snatched it away. Then he backed, as swiftly; and it was obvious that he had trained himself never to risk being attacked. He stood further back than he had, and read the letter under one of the dim lamps.

So, here was Dutch Himmy.

Here was the man whom New York knew as well as Chicago had once known Al Capone. Here was the man who could even confine the activities of Cy Day - and whose reputation could stretch out long arms and scare a little homesteader like Tim Mellish. There he was in person, his face behind the mask, head covered, hat brim pulled down, shapeless raincoat hiding his figure. He was no more than six feet away from the Toff.

A man stood at each side of the Toff, both armed, and there wasn't much doubt about what would happen if he leapt; and yet - what kind of blessing would it be if he could kill Dutch Himmy?

He had never been a man with illusions.

He knew that there was a sound chance that they didn't intend to let him get away alive; if they thought he had dangerous knowledge, they would kill him.

Forget it; wait; win more time. He had made a good start, hadn't he? He had given a truthful answer, and it was demonstrably true.

Dutch Himmy lowered the letter.

"What did he say in the cable?" he asked, flatly.

"Just asked if I was free."

"Did he name anyone?"

"No."

"That true?"

"All he told me was in that letter," Rollison said.

"Did he telephone you from New York?"

"No."

"All right," Dutch Himmy said, "and it had better be true." He seemed to have relaxed, in those few seconds; as if he had been reassured by the letter he'd read - and that meant that one of his great fears had been that Wilf Hall had named him. Therefore, Wilf Hall knew him. Easy. Kindergarten. Wilf Hall knew or suspected the identity of Dutch Himmy, and in one way that could be a help. Wilf Hall probably knew five hundred people reasonably well, and thousands by sight, but - it was a help. If the police could start working on that angle, they might get results which had been denied them before. How to let the police know was a matter to deal with later.

Dutch said, in his hard voice: "Did you shoot Al Cadey?"

"Who?"

"Cadey. In the apartment on 13th Street."

Rollison said slowly, suspiciously: "No. But Cadey had it coming; he was trying to get too personal with Valerie Hall."

"Who shot him?"

"That's a question I don't answer," Rollison said, flatly.

The man who had named Dutch Himmy moved forward restlessly.

"Dutch, I . . ."

"When I want help I'll tell you." That was a reproof. "Rollison, you can start thinking again! I want answers. Where did you take Valerie Hall?"

That was a shot in the dark, of course; it couldn't be anything else. But it made Rollison's heart contract, and he hoped that his voice was steady when he answered:

"Where did I take her? You're crazy. I thought you"

"You took her away from the Belle Hotel."

"You're dreaming," Rollison said, and his voice grew loud. "You". He broke off, and raised his hands, as if imploringly: "Didn't you kidnap her?"

He sounded aghast; bewildered.

Dutch Himmy stood two yards in front of him, staring out of those empty eye-holes. There was a change in the mood; a change in all of them. This was the crisis point. Whatever else he had done wrong, he knew that he had been right in reasoning that above everything else, Dutch Himmy needed to find Valerie; that while she was missing, the man was stymied. That was half-way good.

If he felt sure that Rollison knew where to find her, that wasn't good at all. That would mean they would stop at nothing at all to make him talk.

"Rollison," Dutch Himmy said, "I know you took her away. Don't keep me waiting. Where is she?"

18

LONG DROP

AFTER Dutch Himmy's last question, there was silence. In it, Rollison knew that he had gained little, except the time to think. They wouldn't let him go. Dutch Himmy knew that he could tell him the one thing that he wanted to know. No one got a reputation like Dutch Himmy's without good reason. A man could be a hero and still give way to the kind of questioning that would come now - if Rollison couldn't prevent it from happening.

He must.

He could not answer this man, either for Valerie's sake or for the Mellish family, but ...

He just sat there, as if stubbornly.

He knew now exactly what he would have to do. He must put up a good show of defiance, no matter how much punishment he had to take, and then appear to give way. He would put Dutch Himmy on to a false trail, and before the truth was discovered he would have to make his chance to get away.

"Dutch ..." began the man who spoke most.

"If you don't tell me, Toff," Dutch Himmy said, "I'll turn the men loose on you."

"What do you think I am?" Rollison asked roughly. "I came here to look after the girl, not to hand her over to a brute like you."

There was a moment of stillness, as of amazement; and then one man's hand moved, to punch him in the ribs - and he leapt forward. He beat them by a fraction of a second. He struck Dutch Himmy on the side of the face and sent him sprawling. He felt the papier mache of the mask give way. A man hacked at his legs, and he dodged. Another came bodily at him, and he swerved to one side, handed the man off, and made for the elevator. The doors stood open so invitingly. He was only two yards away when two men barred his path, and another caught up with him from behind, hand at his injured shoulder. He turned and drove his right fist into a yielding face, and for a moment he was free again. But the way to the elevator was still barred. He hardly knew what he was doing when he ran towards the windows. Shadowy figures were coming in the other direction, to head him off, but for those seconds he was free.

He reached a window.

Back to it, he could fight ...

He thrust a hand out, to save himself from stumbling into the window, and the window wasn't there. The glass was only a few inches above the waist-high wall, for the window opened by winding, as the window of a car; and it was open now. His hand felt no resistance at all. He lurched forward. For a dreadful moment, all the lights of New York seemed to be coming up to meet him, it seemed as if he were going to plunge headlong past a hundred and one storeys to the deadly street below.

He didn't.

He came up against the wall itself, at waist height. It jolted the breath out of him, and spelt the end of his sortie. He felt the man grab him, swing him round - and then the avalanche came. Through it all, he held on desperately to one cause for hope; they would not kill him until he told them where to find Valerie.

He covered up as best he could. It seemed as if they were

driving him round the promenade of the tower, not once but a dozen times. Yet he was still conscious when they stopped and he was pushed into the chair again, gasping for breath, lips and nose bloody, body aching. They splashed water over him, and then one of them held his head back and gave him a drink of rye whisky from a flask. It stung the cut lips badly, and he writhed, but soon it began to help, and soon he could see again.

And he could hear.

The hard voice was as free from emotion as ever.

"Rollison," Dutch Himmy said, "save yourself trouble and tell us where to find the girl."

Rollison didn't answer.

"Dutch . . ." the agitator began,

"Hold it."

There was a long pause. Dutch seemed to be staring at Rollison. His own breathing became steadier. The ring of men was close and more threatening, as if they meant to make quite sure that he didn't try another leap for the elevator, and he could see the silhouettes of two men close to it.

He felt a breath of wind, now; from the window. Of course, the windows were open at one side because it was so hot - already it was too warm. Remember, there was an open window. Remember that he had to do one of two things: fool them about Valerie, or get away in time to save himself from further hurt.

"I'll ask you just once more," Dutch Himmy said, "and after that you'll really know big trouble. Where is Valerie Hall?"

The agitator took his wrist and began to twist; and he knew that the man could break his arm. He knew what else they could do, too: break finger by finger. He began to struggle. The pressure grew tighter, the pain worse. He began to sweat and to writhe. Dutch Himmy stood there like a faceless man, and other shadowy figures watched, until suddenly Rollison screamed:

"Don't do it, don't do it, I'll tell you!"

The man released him, slowly.

In that hard voice, Dutch Himmy said: "Okay, where is she? It had better be true."

Rollison gasped: "It's the truth! I - I took her to a friend on Long Island, place near Rockville Centre, she..."

Dutch Himmy said very thinly:

"I know you didn't. You went through the Holland Tunnel and you came back across the George Washington Bridge. You didn't have time to get to Long Island after that. You don't seem to understand," he went on; "I'm going to make you tell me where to find Valerie Hall. That's the beginning and the end. Once you've told me, you'll be through with the punishment. While you lie about it, you'll get so much punishment you won't know which part of you is bone and which part is muscle." The man paused, and then went on in the same hard voice: "Lew, you got that thumbscrew?"

"Sure."

"Show him we mean business."

"Sure" the man named Lew said, as if he had been waiting for this.

One of them gripped Rollison from behind, the other took his right arm and thrust it forward, holding it in such a way that he couldn't turn his wrist. He felt metal. He knew that it wouldn't be long before they showed what they could do. He knew that he wouldn't be able to stand the pressure much longer without breaking down.

He gasped.

"Give me - give me some air!" He had to pretend he felt suffocated, that he could hardly breathe. "I'll tell you, but give me some air." He was gulping and gasping, and they slackened their hold, and looked at Dutch Himmy for orders. "It's so hot in here; I'm choking." Rollison gasped. "I'll tell you, but give me some air!"

He could imagine Dutch Himmy asking himself: "Where's the risk?" There were the open windows, a hundred and one floors above the street; there were two men guarding the elevators; there wasn't anything that any man could do.

The screw was firm, not tight, on Rollison's thumb.

He swayed, as if he was going to pass out, and that made the decision for them. At a word from the man in the mask, he was taken towards the window. Wind came off the rivers and off Long Island Sound, bathing Rollison's face. They didn't need to hold him, for there was just no way that he could escape; they made a semi-circle about him, waiting for him to recover.

If they broke him sufficiently, he would tell them where Valerie was.

Face it; there were limits to human endurance.

When he had told them, they would kill him.

There was no reason why they should let him live.

He leaned against the window, as if he was taking in great gulps of air, and he gripped the top of the wall tightly. He could feel the slot where the glass went, quite distinctly. He didn't look down to the street level. He saw that from here there was a sloping wall, which went ten or twelve storeys down, to a ledge wide enough for a man to stand on; for a car to stand on! If he fell, the ledge might save him. If he didn't . . .

He swung himself out of the window, before they could stop him.

The ledge saved him.

As he found his feet, he went sideways, crabwise, until a buttress hid him from the men at the windows. He had taken them so completely by surprise that they had let him get out of range.

He was out here, a hundred and one storeys up; alone.

The corner of the top of the Atyeo Building was only twenty feet away from Rollison, and he edged towards it. He had his back to the wall below the windows of the Observation Tower, and his arms spread wide, for balance. Those blessed buttresses saved him. If he toppled forward, there wouldn't be a chance, but at least he needn't fear Dutch Himmy's men - yet.

He couldn't climb down, but could he climb up?

He didn't think of Valerie, or of the reasons for what he had done. His head was swimmy, but not with fear. He felt a kind of exultation; ecstasy. He was here alone, at the top of the world, at the top of wonderland. He was edging towards the corner and to a spot even further away from the men at the tower windows. He didn't give them much thought, either. Time passed slowly; or at least, it seemed to.

If anything was certain, it was that no one would follow him with any eagerness; they might revolt even against Dutch Himmy if he ordered them to risk falling a thousand feet or more.

Some windows were in sight, and suddenly a head appeared.

An arm appeared, next.

The starlight showed Rollison close to the wall, and fell upon the man's gun. Well, that was reasonable; they wouldn't want him to live; if they fired at him they could make sure that he went down there, to crash to his death. Just a little wound would be enough; even if he flinched, he would slip.

There was a word; it sounded like: "Don't." Don't what? The head and the arm and the gun disappeared. Rollison was very close to the corner now, out of sight of all the windows. The sense of exultation had never been greater. He was on top of the world, lord of all he surveyed, and they had not shot at him. Reprieve, again.

Somewhere, deep in his consciousness, he knew that he was drunk with a kind of fatalism.

He was close to the corner.

A man leaned out again, and his head and arm moved - and he was throwing something. Throwing. Whatever it was missed Rollison by inches, and struck the wall. He pressed close to the wall, cowering now, his mood changed for a split second; and then it changed back, and he could have laughed aloud. They'd missed. They'd thrown ...

Something struck him on the shoulder.

It didn't hurt, but it made him flinch, and his right foot

slipped.

His right leg went down.

He cried out in awful dread, and tried to clutch the wall, but couldn't. He felt as if the rainbow land below was pulling him, making sure that he went down.

But he clutched the ledge with both hands and then fought to get his foot back on it. He was so close to the corner that he could surely edge his way round. They couldn't get at him there without climbing out, and he felt quite sure that they would never do that.

He felt a blow at his shoulder. This time, he didn't flinch. The 'thing' they'd thrown went clattering down, until it faded into silence.

Now, he was at the corner - there were no windows above him, and he was protected by the buttresses from anything the men threw at him. Safe.

He stood there, almost silly with relief. The wind was stronger here, and he was too cold; shivering. He couldn't control his shivers. He leaned back, with his eyes closed, hot and cold in turn and shivering violently, wondering what would happen if an extra vicious spasm shook him. Not wondering, knowing. That ledge, that sea of light.

He stopped shivering.

He opened his eyes, and realised that it was lighter here than he had expected; there was a kind of flood-lighting - of course, flood-lighting. Then, he rounded the corner in the other direction, and a great light shone upon him, so fierce that it seemed to pin him to the wall.

Here, the ledge was wider.

And behind him was a door.

19

THE DOOR

At first, Rollison was shocked into paralysed stillness. Then, he turned to look more closely at the door. It was in the stone wall. There were no windows, just the door itself. He could tell that it had been put there so that workmen could attend to the flood-lighting at this corner. The flood-lights were at each of the four corners; he remembered: seeing that from below. There would be a flight of stairs leading from this platform, and Dutch Himmy's men would know about it; if they didn't, they would soon find out.

He had a little room to move, now, and stood back very cautiously. There was a metal handle to the door, and a large keyhole. This would be a favourite place for suicides, wouldn't it? No one would want to leave that key in the lock; whoever was in charge would make sure that it could only be obtained by authorised people. Obviously. So, the door would be locked. He had a little time. He had just as much time as it would take Dutch Himmy's men to find the staircase and to pick the lock. It wasn't likely to be very complicated, but he kicked against something.

He stood suddenly still, fearful of overbalancing; but he was quite safe. He looked down at his feet. There was a small coil of electric cable, here to feed the flood-lights - a spare piece which must have been left behind by work men. Rubber-covered cable, just a yard or so of it. What use. . . .

He heard a sound, from the door.

He couldn't be absolutely sure, but believed that it was being pushed; or pulled. Men would push and pull if they were trying to open it, wouldn't they? So he hadn't long now - he could take it for granted that there would be at least one expert cracksman in the crowd with Dutch Himmy.

How . . .

He bent down suddenly, grabbed the wire, uncoiled it, and went towards the door. There was a narrow gap at the top and bottom and at the sides. He bent down and pushed the two ends of the wire between the bottom of the door and the floor; that would jam the door, would gain him more precious minutes, but - it wouldn't keep them in.

Down below, a hopeless distance below, were people, cars, taxis, policemen, laughter, security. A hundred and one floors, nearly twelve hundred feet. And almost directly opposite him was another tall building, with an observation tower and a blue light above it; blue floodlighting, against the white which was here.

Could he be seen?

If anyone was in that other tower, would they see him?

He must make them see him.

Rollison did not really think; most of the things he did were born of desperation. There was really no hope, so he made hope. He had the Night Telegram in his pocket; a few pages. He had his lighter. He took sheets of the Night Telegram and his heart was cheered, because there were a lot of sheets; twenty or thirty of them. The wind blew, steadily. He screwed up two sheets and put them close to the wall, as far away from the flood-light as he could. The light itself was shining on the top of the tower, not straight at him. He bent down, hid the lighter in his hands, and flicked it. He put the quivering flame to the newspaper, and it caught at once.

It went out.

He licked his lips.

He could hear the distant throbbing sounds of the streets, now; and he could also hear the nearer, thudding noise as they worked at the door. Once they got to him out here, he would not even have the beginning of a chance. He nicked again, and held the lighter under the newspaper for a longer period, and it flared up.

He backed away from the tongue of flame.

The wind got beneath the paper and lifted it, and the blazing paper floated, like a burning crown, slowly and gracefully above Rollison's head. Then, still burning, it floated towards the other tall building, brilliant in the darkness.

"They'll see it," Rollison said in a strangled voice; "they're bound to see it!"

He lit another piece, and held it as it flamed and then tossed it high; another and another. At one time, three burning crowns were floating through the air. The smell of smoke wafted back to him, strong and astringent; somehow like heady wine. After each piece floated away, he stared at the door; and he could see it shivering, knew that Dutch Himmy's men were putting all their weight into the effort. Only the cable kept it closed, now - the door itself was open half an inch.

He lit the last piece of newspaper. It floated away, into silence, and the flames seemed to go towards the stars. He looked down at the distant city. There was a turmoil of movement down there as cars went along the ribbon-like streets and ants crawled along the pavements; it was like a giant in slow motion.

No one looked up.

That was, he didn't see anyone look up; he couldn't be sure. But he told himself grimly that, had they noticed him, there would have been a crowd gaping and craning their necks, evidence he could not have failed to see.

They were so distant; aloof; in a different world. His world was the loneliness of the sky and the gentle wind and the thudding sound of the banging against the door. The last spark of the last blaze died away. He saw a few small pieces of black ash floating near him, that was all; the charred wreckage of his hopes.

He looked at the door.

He knew what was inevitable, now, and seemed to realise that the ecstasy had been a fantasy. There had never been a chance.

He tried to make up his mind what to do next.

Then, into the quiet, there came a sharp ringing sound; an alarming termagant of a noise. He couldn't understand; it was as if a fire-engine had climbed a hundred storeys and was ringing just below him. But there were no bells in New York, were there? Didn't they have sirens? He listened again, and the sound was still there, a harsh brr-brr-brr-brr.

The thudding had stopped.

The ringing stopped, and into the hush a man said: "This is Lew."

There was another pause.

Rollison knew what it was now; a telephone bell, and Lew was answering the call. Lew the agitator. Lew had been one of those pushing. Rollison went closer to the door, and he heard Lew say in a harsh voice:

"We've got visitors."

Dutch Himmy said roughly: "Let's have it."

"The cops."

"What?"

"The cops," Lew said, in a stony voice. "That's Midge talking. Rollison attracted attention somehow. We've got to scram."

A man echoed: "We've got to scram?"

"We've time to push Rollison over the edge," Lew said, and there was another lull - and then a scuffle of feet, as if men were moving hurriedly, and finally the tugging at the door again. Rollison saw it quivering. He saw that the piece of cable was moving. He made an involuntary move towards the door, but before he reached it his knee gave way underneath him. He stumbled. Light came on and shone out towards him, and behind the light there was a shadow.

Lew.

Here was Lew, with an automatic in his hand, sidling through the doorway, cautious although he knew that Rollison had no gun. His hand, arm and one foot appeared. Retreat was useless. Rollison, upright and close to the wall, sidled towards Lew. If he could snatch at the gun before Lew saw him -

Lew said: "Give yourself up, Toff."

Rollison didn't answer.

"Give yourself up, Toff," Lew said again. "Come down with us; that's the one chance you have of living. Come and tell us where to find the girl, and you'll be okay."

Rollison kept silent, still edging towards the door. He was sweating now, and could feel the sweat running down his forehead and into his eyes.

"It's your one chance," Lew said.

Rollison was close enough to snatch at the gun. He struck out, and knocked it out of Lew's grasp - but he had made one miscalculation, hadn't given the ruse a thought. As the gun fell, Lew thrust himself into sight, big and powerful and with another gun in his left hand.

He jerked it up.

"Okay, Toff!" he cried.

He fired.

Rollison went for the man's knees.

The bullet went over his head, and the flash was swallowed up by the flood-lights. Rollison felt his hands touch Lew's legs, and he pulled savagely. Pain screeched through his shoulder, but he brought Lew down. He knew that the other man was fresh and unhurt, that even if everything was equal he would have no more than a fifty-fifty chance. Now, if he counted the odds, he had no chance at all, for Lew's hands were already at his neck.

They were close to the edge.

Rollison got a hold on Lew's arm, made the supreme effort, and pulled.

Lew flew over him; fell on the ledge and then, after a split second of awful silence, went over, screaming.

Rollison lay still.

There were the footsteps of several men; voices; questions. Then, men came through the open doorway and saw him. He knew they were there. He saw that they were policemen. He had no strength to speak to them, just lay still. The scream was still echoing in his ears.

He came round, without knowing whether he'd lost consciousness, or been asleep, or been doped. He was lying still. He felt more ache than pain in one knee, in his left shoulder, and beneath his jaw. He knew that he did not want to move; that he was snug and warm, and that there was no danger. He might have been floating somewhere between earth and heaven.

He dozed off again.

Next time he came round, he knew that he was comfortable, he could smell antiseptics, he was prepared to open his eyes and see a nurse. In fact, the ward was empty. There were flowers, which surprised him. There were pictures on the walls, and yet he was sure that it wasn't a room in an ordinary house. By his side were the usual things: thermometer, temperature chart - everything to suggest that he had been seriously ill.

Nonsense?

He felt as if he had been.

He felt warm and snug and content to lie there, and knew that was enough to prove that he wasn't normal. He had no desire to move. He was only mildly curious about what had happened, and where he was, but gradually memory came back. Dutch and the other man, Lew, and ... Dutch Himmy.

A scream, cops, men smashing at him with fists and feet, burning crowns, charred paper, a scream, threats, questions and cops and - Valerie.

Was Valerie all right? The question was like a sword-thrust.

He opened his eyes wider, and saw the bell-push by the side

of the bed. He had hardly pressed it when the door opened and a man came in, a man who seemed to have dogged him since he had first telephoned Cy Day. It was Legs Leggatt. Legs wore a pale blue suit and his dark hair was shiny with pomade, his thin face was set in a grin which was undoubtedly meant to be amiable.

"Hi," he greeted.

"Hi," returned Rollison, and left it at that.

Legs said: "Anything you want?"

"Just information."

"About who?"

"Valerie Hall."

"Wherever you hid her, you hid her," said Legs; "no one has seen or heard of her since you went mountaineering. How does it feel to die?"

"Better ask those who know," Rollison said. "Is that true about Valerie?"

"On the level."

"Thanks," said Rollison. "Thanks, Legs."

"You feeling up to visitors?" asked Legs, "because the Boss said that when you were able to talk, he would come right over. He fixed to have you brought here so that he could keep an eye on you, and the police and Cy are like that, so it was okay. Ready to talk?"

"Yes," Rollison said without enthusiasm. "I suppose so."

"Fine," said Legs. "I'll send for Cy." He moved towards the door. "Sure there's nothing you want to drink?"

"Later, thanks," said Rollison. "There are people I'd like to hear about. My taxi-driver . . ."

"He's on his feet again," said Legs; "they nearly split his skull, but he had it steel-lined."

Rollison felt relief coursing through him.

"Fine. And Russell?"

"He's okay," Legs said. "Just mad. So mad he's almost crazy; if he ever finds Dutch Himmy" Legs broke off. "Forget it."

"Thanks," Rollison said.

"Okay." Legs went out, and the door closed quietly.

So he was at the Belle Hotel, where Valerie had been, Rollison reasoned. It was as good a place as any. Probably Cy Day and the police had agreed that he was better here than anywhere else; he could at least be watched. He sat up. For the first time, he saw the newspapers in an open cupboard by the side of the bed, and he took them. He didn't open them at first, but pushed back the bedclothes, and started to get out of bed. He staggered and nearly fell. He got back and leaned against the pillows, breathing hard. It was fully five minutes before he felt normal again; and even then he wasn't really normal, for his knee and his shoulder had started to throb.

He didn't try to get out again.

A nurse came in, angular, with a sharp face and a twinkle in green eyes, and she straightened the pillow, took his temperature, did all the things which should have been infuriating, but weren't. Then she fetched him a glass of warm milk, and he was surprised that he not only enjoyed it, he wanted it. Then she propped him up.

"Now you look well enough to meet the Boss," she said, and stared at him from the foot of the bed.

"I wondered what the fuss was about," said Rollison dryly. "Tell me something."

"I haven't any spare dates."

"You've a lot of self-confidence," Rollison said, and gave a faint grin. "Who sent the flowers?"

The nurse laughed.

"Don't raise your hopes, Toff; they're from Tim as well as Mary."

The smile faded from Rollison's face. The nurse realised that what she said went much deeper than she had meant, and moved quickly towards him, as if he were in need of help. He didn't know that he lost what little colour he had, and that he looked dreadfully afraid.

"How - how did they ..." he began, and then had the sense

to stop. Let no one know where Valerie was, give no one a clue. Perhaps he'd already given this nurse one. He must say something; something. "How did anyone know so soon?" he muttered.

"News gets around in three days," the nurse said. She stood and watched as if wondering what the effect of that would be.

20

FACTS ABOUT WILF

THREE days ...

Rollison looked intently at the nurse, then at the window and the drawn blinds, then at the newspapers. After the first shock, he glanced again at the newspapers. There was the Night Telegram for four nights in a row, starting at the night he already knew. There were the New York Herald Tribune and the Mirror for three days. On the first, the headlines were of the rescue from the top of the Atyeo Building. There was his photograph - a studio portrait doubtless supplied by Cy Day and a picture of him on the edge of the first floor - another of him being put into an ambulance. He looked like something out of the jungle. In the Mirror and the Night Telegram there were pictures of what was left of Lew. There were reconstruction stories which reached the heights of improbability, but there was one significant thing; only the Night Telegram mentioned Dutch Himmy and that simply in passing.

Police, he was given to understand, were watching by his bedside.

He found himself smiling, twistedly. Cy and the police worked as closely as anyone could.

"Think I can leave you, now?" the nurse asked.

He blew her a kiss.

He glanced through several of the newspapers, and then leaned back and closed his eyes. He was much more tired than he had expected to be, and was glad to relax. He hoped Cy would give him a little time to recover. Three days on his back was a clear indication that he had been in a bad way. He wondered if anything was broken, and how long he would have to stay here. He was so numbed that he didn't really care, and hardly gave a thought to three lost days.

A doctor came, but Rollison was tired again, and soon slept. It was two days before he was anything like himself.

When he woke up, it was dark outside and a small lamp burned in a corner. He felt much better. He even wondered how many more days had passed since he had last come round, and began to feel anxious about the time that was passing, and the fact that Dutch Himmy was still able to look for Valerie. There was that nagging worry, too; that Valerie might have been found since he had asked Legs.

There was a tap at the door. First a doctor and nurse came, and he submitted to the examination, was told that he was lucky, but would do. Later, a different, elderly nurse came in, and said quietly:

"You've some visitors; the doctor's approved of that."

"That's fine," Rollison said, and nearly meant it.

She helped him to sit up; helped him. He was glad of it. He was comfortable. He knew that he was unshaven, but it didn't matter. He remembered what had happened when he had first come round, and he looked for the newspapers again; the only addition were two more Night Telegrams and Mirrors, so only hours had passed. He heard nothing, but the door opened, and he realised for the first time that the room was sound-proof.

Cy Day and two other men came in; tall, powerful-looking men, one of them a young Adonis, the other more like a veteran of the Seven Seas. Cy introduced them - Captain Morris and Sergeant Hannington of the Homicide Bureau. They had a 'few' questions to ask. In fact, the veteran began to ask them and the sergeant took notes. The questions came easily and smoothly, almost to pattern; how had it all started, and why?

Rollison told them everything; that he had left the Milwest Hotel, and Brian Conway and Halloran, with Russell and walked into trouble. There was nothing he needed to keep back. Morris made it obvious, in his slow-speaking way, that he now knew that Wilf Hall had been kidnapped, that there had been talk of ransom; so there was little that Rollison felt hesitant about. He'd been to see Conway and Halloran because he thought they might know how to get to Dutch Himmy.

He told them about how Quentin had died in Valerie's arms; and what he had done.

He told them about the visit to Cadey, but not that Conway had shot the man.

As he talked on, his head began to swim, and his voice grew hoarse. He was glad when the door opened and the nurse came in; equally glad that Morris didn't argue. They let him rest again. But it wasn't a long rest; not as long as he wanted, for when he came round again, there they were, and Morris started more questioning. His quiet, pleasant voice was disarming; he put his questions as if he had been examining witnesses all his life.

Probably he had.

And then came the question which Rollison had been waiting for:

"Where is Miss Hall, will you tell me?" Morris had small, dark blue and very bright eyes; smiling and friendly.

Rollison said: "No."

"We can make a big job of searching for her," said Morris; "she might be able to hide from Dutch Himmy, but she can't hide from us."

"If you want to find out where she is, you look," Rollison said, "and if Dutch Himmy finds and harms her, you tell your children how proud you are about it."

Morris was smiling faintly; amusedly.

"If we don't know where she is, we can't protect her."

"That's right," said Rollison.

"Do you know where she is?"

Rollison said: "I'm beginning to wonder."

Morris changed the subject with a grin which seemed to say: "We'll come back to it soon. You'll never hold out." He asked: "Mr. Rollison, what did Dutch Himmy look like? Can you help us to identify him?"

"Not very much," Rollison said, and told him what he could. The handsome young sergeant made more notes, and Morris asked a few quick additional questions; none of them helped. Finished, he leaned back and said with a one-sided smile:

"You're the only man I've ever spoken to who claims to have seen and spoken to Dutch Himmy," he said; "and that's a good reason why we think your life's in danger."

Rollison didn't speak.

Morris went on: "We picked up what there was left of the man who fell over the edge, Mr. Rollison. Papers in his possession showed that he was a Lew Anderson, living in the Bronx. We're finding out all we can about him, but in five days we haven't found much. Can you give us any further help?"

"There was a man they called Midge."

"Midge," Morris echoed, and shot a glance at the sergeant. "Midge," he repeated. "Fine. That might help." He stood up, and stretched. "Mr. Rollison, you've done plenty that makes you a hero, but" - his smile was as charming as a smile could be - "you won't find the police in New York so obliging as they are in London. We don't know you so well. I'm just giving you time to think things over. Remember we want to know where Valerie Hall is."

"Captain, I don't want you to think I like playing a hero, but I took a lot of punishment refusing to answer that question when Dutch Himmy put it to me," Rollison said. "You can use what pressure you like, but it won't make me give that away. Don't take that personally. I just don't trust anyone in the wide, wide world."

Throughout all of this, Cy Day had sat looking on and listening, but not saying a word. He stood up as Morris turned and went out, with the sergeant behind him. He closed the door on them, and then turned and looked down at Rollison, his full lips puckering. He lit a cigarette and handed it to Rollison, who took it and said:

"Thanks."

"Rolly," Day said, "you'll have to trust the police sooner or later."

"Perhaps," said Rollison.

"How is it going to help if you keep quiet?"

"Cy," said Rollison, "I don't want the wrong people to know where Valerie is." His voice was very quiet and his gaze steady; and he went on bluntly: "We've known each other a long time."

"Sure. Whatever you think, you can tell me."

"I'm getting ready to. You had all your leg-men out to look for me when I took Valerie away. You covered the city. I slipped you, but it wasn't your fault. You screened Sikorski for me, and that meant that you had reports of all my movements. You've known more about what I've been doing than anyone else since I came to New York. You knew - Legs Leggatt made that obvious - that I'd been to New Jersey, that I went out through the Holland Tunnel and came back over the George Washington Bridge. Is that right?"

"It's right."

"Dutch Himmy knew that, too," said Rollison. "That's why I don't trust anybody."

All that Cy Day did was to take the cigar from his lips, glance at the ash, and then look back at Rollison.

They were silent for several minutes.

There was no sound from outside - in the street or in the hotel.

It seemed as if each was determined to wait until the other broke the silence.

Cy Day did.

Cy Day stood up, smiled faintly, and put his cigar down on the ashtray. He looked very big. He was dressed in a pale brown suit which fitted perfectly. In his way, he was handsome; perhaps just a little too obviously prosperous, a little too much like Wall Street; that was all.

"If there's one thing I like," he said, "it's talk straight from the shoulder. Do I look like Dutch Himmy to you?"

"You're too big." Rollison smiled. "Physically."

"Thanks."

"Cy," said Rollison, softly, "that's being smart. This isn't a thing to be smart about. Perhaps I sound ungrateful. Perhaps I've annoyed you. Well, if that annoys you I can't help it - there's a lot at stake. I can't afford to make any more mistakes. I'm telling you that within an hour or two of my return to New York, Dutch Himmy knew the way I went and the way I came back. Either he had a man watching me and followed me both ways - which no one did - or he got a report. Legs greeted me near the George Washington Bridge, and knew plenty. How far do you trust Legs Leggatt?"

"All my operatives are reliable," Cy said.

"So reliable that I won't tell you or anyone else where to find Valerie Hall," Rollison said, "and if you want me to say I'm sorry, okay, I'm sorry."

Day was still smiling, faintly.

"I wouldn't have you any different," he said. "All right, Rolly, there could be a leakage my end. I can't swear that I haven't an operator who won't squeal if the corn is ripe enough. Not Legs - Legs is much too good and safe. And since you've been laid up here, he's been busy."

"Looking for Valerie?"

"No, doing what I promised you - tracing Wilf's last movements." When Rollison's eyes quickened with interest, Day went on: "Here's good for evil. I'll tell you what Legs has found out about Wilf. His last known movements. Ready?"

"Waiting," Rollison said eagerly.

"Fine. He was at the Arden-Astoria two hours before he set out for Idlewild Airport. He wasn't followed, as far as we know. He ran low on gas on the other side of the Queensborough Bridge. They were only using the lower level that night, the higher level was being repaired. You know what it's like coming down off the lower level. Not much traffic about, the big arches, one of the darkest parts of New York. There was a nearby gas station where he pulled in for gas. They filled his tank, and then found that it had a leak. He hired another car from that gas station, and from there he was followed. He didn't go straight towards the main highway and Idlewild, he probably tried to dodge his pursuers, because he must have known that something was wrong by then. The car he hired was found half a mile from the gas station. It was in a wrecker's yard, and it wasn't until last night that we found it. Like to know what we found in it?"

Rollison caught his breath.

"Not - Wilf?"

"No," said Cy Day, quietly, "not Wilf, but a lot of dried blood."

21
MAN ON HIS FEET

ROLLISON was silent for a long time; for minutes. He was trying to see not only what this could mean to Valerie, but its significance from the very beginning. Had Wilf been killed that first night? If so, why? Would a man kill and then demand a ransom? Weren't they likely to keep him alive for a while, so as to be able to prove that he was alive if proof was needed? A living victim was more likely to yield big dividends than a dead one.

Dried blood could mean a fight; injury; or death in that car.

"You wouldn't know Wilf's blood group, would you?" asked Rollison, at last.

"Group O, but that doesn't mean much - it's the largest. Like the group of the blood in the car."

"Nothing else found?"

"No."

"Anything discovered from Dando or Russell?"

"Nothing more. They just get mad. Since Russell discovered that his partner had been murdered, he's been" Day hesitated, and stood up, waving his hands.

"Well, he's behaving as if he's lost everything."

"Just what happened after I left him?"

Day grinned. "That's a way to put it! He was knocked out

and bundled into a doorway, and when he came round, everything was over. He got a cab and went straight home - and his sister says that she can hardly get a word out of him. He's not badly hurt, but"

Day hesitated."It was just a case of David and Jonathan with him and Mark Quentin."

"What made Russell go to see Conway?"

"You'd named Conway, and Russell simply lost his self-control when he heard about Quentin."

"Dando didn't look after him very well," Rollison said, dryly.

"Dando's doing his own job - for the Night Telegram as well as for Dando himself. Russell was just one of the people who might help. So were you. Dando"

Cy Day waved his hands again as he searched for words - "Dando's crazy about one thing: finding Dutch Himmy. He's been at the door downstairs five or six times a day. He's been told that you're unconscious, but now he's seen Morris and me come in he'll know that you can talk. Want to see him?"

"I've no objection."

"Give yourself a rest first," advised Day. "Morris is enough to wear anyone out, and then you've had me to deal with. Anything else you want to know?"

"Cy," said Rollison,"I'd like you to keep tags on Conway and Halloran, on Dando and on Legs Leggatt - and anyone else you think might be of interest. That's one. Then I'd like you to look for any reason why Wilf Hall should be murdered; not kidnapped, murdered. If we can get a motive . . ."

"I was born,- too," Day said.

Rollison grinned.

"Fine, we both know about motives! And then we need to screen all the people who knew Wilf. That's quite a job, but it may be the only way to get results. I told Morris, and I wasn't joking, that Dutch Himmy's one great fear was that Wilf might have named him in his other identity. There's reason to believe that Wilf knew or knows who he was - and that could be motive enough in itself. If Wilf was going to talk" He broke off, shrugging. "Can you think of a better motive?"

"Yes," said Day, and smiled easily.

"Well, if you prefer to keep it to yourself, I couldn't blame you," Rollison said.

"We can share it. The police know it. Wilf Hall is Big Business. Wilf Hall bought the Atyeo Building. Wilf Hall has a lot of enemies, in the way that all successful men have. Find someone who hates his guts, someone he's given a raw deal. I don't say it happened that way, but you asked for another motive."

"Thanks," said Rollison.

Day went nearer to him. "Rolly," he said, "who don't you trust? Legs - or me?"

Rollison eyed him steadily for a long time, then said very softly: "Sorry, Cy. There's just one man in the wide, wide world I trust at this moment."

"Meaning, the Toff."

"That's the man."

"Toff," said Day, smiling only faintly, "sometimes I think you're the biggest big-head the world's ever known. Sometimes I think you're just crazy. Sometimes I think you ought to get the Victoria Cross and the Purple Heart on the same day. And sometimes I think you're dead right. This is one of the times when I think you're dead right. I don't like admitting it even to myself, but what you told me about Dutch Himmy's knowledge of the way you left Manhattan and the way you came back, has shaken me badly. I'm going to comb my own operatives, starting now. And I'm going to work on this as I've never worked on a job before. And when it's over, you're going to buy me the best dinner in New York, and say 'sorry' with each course."

He went out.

The nurse and the doctor would not allow Dando to see the Toff that day.

Dando came, next morning. He asked a lot of questions, but

he had nothing new to say. The newspapers had banner headlines about the discovery of the car which Wilf Hall had hired, the fact that the petrol tank in his own car had been holed pointed straight to a plot to delay him. There were stories, none of them really reliable, that Wilf had been afraid of trouble for a long time.

Dando said: "You're the only man alive, as far as we know, who's ever talked to Dutch Himmy. That makes you precious to a lot of people, especially to Russell and to me. Be careful when you're ready to leave here, Toff."

"I'll be careful," Rollison promised.

There was a succession of visitors. Morris and his sergeant again, Cy Day, Dando, other newspapermen, friends who had known him in England, Morris again, doctors, nurses - and these, Rollison knew, were now largely superfluous; Morris and Cy were deliberately playing up his injuries, and making out that he was worse than he was. Nothing else was discovered. Halloran and Conway stayed at the Milwest Hotel, and still seemed nervous, went out very seldom. The police and Cy Day were going through lists of Wilf Hall's friends and acquaintances; but there were hundreds of them, few with any conceivable motive. The revenge possibility did not reveal any new line.

On the seventh day, Rollison was pronounced well enough to go out, if he took things carefully.

On the ninth day, just before he left the Belle Hotel for a walk, knowing that he would be followed wherever he went, there was another visitor. He saw her from the window of the drawing-room where he had been sitting. She walked briskly. She was very small, her name was Julie, and she was Russell's sister. Even at a distance, there was something about her which won compassion; she looked so nervous, so timid. Rollison felt quite sure that she was here to see him, and went downstairs to greet her. Eagerly. By the time he reached the hall, a bell-boy was speaking to her.

She looked up at Rollison; nervously?

"Hallo, Miss Russell," he said; "come to see me?"

"Yes," she said quickly. "Yes, please. Can I talk to you?"

"Of course. Would you like to talk here or shall we go out?"

"I - I don't mind," she said; "anywhere. It - it's about my brother. I hope you aren't angry with me for coming."

"Not even slightly angry," Rollison assured her. "I'm glad you've come."

It was warm outside, and pleasant, and he had been looking forward to some fresh air. He reminded himself that Cy Day's men would protect him as if he was a Crown Prince. And probably the girl would feel that she could talk freely only when they were out of earshot of anyone else.

Just across the road were the gardens of Riverside Drive, the shade of trees, the cool breeze which came off the river. They strolled out. Cy Day's men were there all right, and one man said:

"Don't do anything without warning us, Mr. Rollison."

"Just a stroll."

"Okay."

A taxi was drawn up not far from the hotel; the nearest vehicle in sight - a red-and-yellow taxi. Rollison glanced across, and Sikoski raised a hand. Rollison waved back and called out: "See you," and then went across the road with the girl. She already seemed more reassured.

"Now, what's the real trouble?" Rollison asked, and his manner and his smile put her completely at her ease.

"It's Van," she said quickly; "I just want to help Van, but he - he's almost crazy. I've never known him anything like it. He says that you're the one man in the world who could identify Dutch Himmy and he's going to make you, somehow." She was breathless again, and she gripped Rollison's arm tightly. "Do you know Dutch Himmy?"

Rollison said: "I wouldn't know him if I saw him."

Her great brown eyes were very near his, and in them he saw the last thing he had expected: relief.

"Thank God for that," she breathed.

Rollison said, startled: "What makes you so thankful?"

"If you knew the man you might tell Van," she said, "and if he knew, then he'd try to kill for himself. I - I just don't want to lose my brother."

Rollison smiled down into that pale face.

"Julie," he said, "if I ever find out who Dutch Himmy is, your brother will be the last man I tell."

Her eyes lit up.

"That's wonderful to hear," she said. "Just wonderful. I've been so worried because of Dando..."

"Why Dando?" Rollison asked, sharply.

Julie said: "I think he's gone mad since - since his brother died." Recollection of the boy she had loved brought tears to her eyes, but she went on: "He's always egging Van on, always telling him that he must find out who Dutch Himmy is. It's Dando who seems sure that you know but won't tell anyone. Van would be bad enough by himself, but with two of them" She broke off. "But if you promise me that..."

Such golden simplicity.

Rollison said: "I'll come and see your brother and try to convince him that I don't know, Julie. Now, supposing we get a taxi for you, and"

He stopped.

He saw the car swing into the road, and tear towards the Belle Hotel. He heard a shout, as of warning, from one of the watching men. He grabbed Julie and flung himself behind some trees, but was a split second too late. There was a burst of shooting. He felt Julie shiver in his arms. As the car roared past and he crouched against the tree, unhurt, she was a dead weight against him.

There was an ugly wound at the back of her head.

Van Russell stood by the window in the living-room of his apartment. Dando was sitting on the arm of a chair. Rollison stood near the door, watching Russell, seeing the way his eyes stormed, his lips worked. All the bandages were gone, now, but his arm was still in a sling. He looked like a man in torment, as if he couldn't control himself.

He had been told that Julie was dead.

"I can't believe it," he said hoarsely, "I just can't believe it; she was so sweet, she was such a honey! Oh, God, why do you let it happen? God, let me find Dutch Himmy, let me avenge her. Let me..."

"Van," Dando said, in a cracked voice, "the man who can help you find Dutch Himmy is right here. He's talked to him, he's seen him. You can believe that line that he couldn't describe the man if you like, but I don't believe it."

Dando stopped; and there was a glitter in his eyes, a lean and hungry look on his face.

Russell moved a step towards the Toff.

"If I thought you knew," he said, and almost choked. "Of course you know. Dando's right; you can put a finger on Dutch Himmy. Come on, name him. Name him! Name the man who's killed my best friend, my sister, who..."

He sounded as if he might burst out screaming.

Rollison said: "Get a hold on yourself; you won't help anyone this way. If I knew Dutch Himmy..."

"But you must know him, you've talked to him," rasped Russell. "And I'm going to make you talk!" He swung round from Rollison, dived towards a small writing-desk and, before Rollison could reach him, snatched out an automatic and covered him. "If you don't name Dutch Himmy I'll shoot you," he threatened savagely. "Who is he?"

22

BACK TO BRIAN CONWAY

RUSSELL was only six feet away. He looked wild enough to shoot to kill. The gun was quivering in his hand, but if he fired the margin of error would be trifling - he couldn't miss. Dando was on his feet now, and Rollison stood quite still. If he jumped or tried to get the gun away he might jolt Russell into shooting.

"Van . . ." Dando began.

"You keep out of this!" Russell flung at him. "Rollison, who is Dutch Himmy?"

Rollison said very softly:

"If I knew, I'd tell you."

"You stood and talked to him, you heard his voice. Even if he wore a mask you heard his voice! What did it sound like? Who is he?"

Rollison said: "He had a very deep voice - you heard that man Halloran, didn't you? Conway's friend."

"I know who you mean. Come on - was that Dutch Himmy? Was he?" Russell almost choked. "Or are you lying to me, are you trying to fob me off?"

"Dutch Himmy's voice was deep, like Halloran's," said Rollison, quietly. "If you ask me, Halloran may know"

Russell swung round.

Rollison swung his arm out, and took the automatic, then

slid it into his own pocket in almost the same movement. He backed away as Russell rounded on him. He wasn't at his peak form, but he was more than a match for the man who seemed to have lost his head.

Dando put in: "Van, why don't you calm down?"

Rollison thrust Russell into a chair, backed away, and said roughly:

"You keep away from Conway, Halloran and Dutch Himmy. You stay here, and get a doctor; if I had my way I'd chain you to the bed until Dutch Himmy's caught. Let me tell you something. Your sister came to see me to plead with me not to tell you who Dutch Himmy was, even if I knew."

Dando exclaimed: "What's that?"

For the first time since he had started to shout, Russell spoke calmly. The rage died out of his eyes, and for a moment he had the look of his sister, and slipped back into his old, almost diffident manner.

"Is that - is that the truth?"

"She came to tell me that she thought you'd get yourself killed if you knew Dutch Himmy, and she begged me not to help you find him. I promised that I wouldn't," Rollison went on, "and that's the kind of promise I don't even think of breaking." He turned round on Dando. "You could spend your time trying to make sure that Dutch Himmy doesn't have any sacrificial victim ready, instead of driving your friend crazy."

Dando said: "So I could," but there was no life in his voice.

Rollison went down to street level. He saw one of Cy Day's men standing just outside the swing doors of the apartment building. It would be easy to go out, cringing, fearful of another attack. He went out briskly, stimulated by the danger; and deeply, bitterly angry. He could picture the dead girl's lovely brown eyes and her eagerness, her delight that he could understand why she had gone to see him, and what she wanted.

Double-parked was Sikoski's cab.

"It's okay," the Agency man said, "no one's about."

"Thanks." Rollison went to the taxi, and got in. Sikoski wasn't grinning, wasn't at all his usual self, but there was no sign of injury on his face. He drove fast until he was on Riverside Drive, and then pulled into the kerb. An Agency car slowed down just behind him. He turned round in his seat, and said thinly:

"You going to be okay?"

"I think so," Rollison said.

No 'Colonel'; no 'Bud'.

"That girl," Sikoski said, and licked his lips. "The way they rubbed her out. That's one thing I'm not going to forget or forgive. The way they killed that girl instead of you. She just happened to get in the way. I guess that's one thing you aren't going to forget or forgive."

"You couldn't be more right," Rollison said. "Did they get the killer?"

"There was a gun battle, and he got his."

"That's a pity," said Rollison. For dead men didn't talk.

There was a buzz of sound in front of Sikoski, who picked up the mouthpiece-cum-earphone of his radio. He said: "Sikoski" and waited, shot a glance at Rollison, and then went on roughly: "Okay, I'll tell him."

He switched the radio off, and turned round towards the Toff. Something in his manner told Rollison that this was even worse than what had happened to Julie Russell. The Toff sat absolutely still, heart hammering, fear sitting at his shoulder.

Sikoski said: "Colonel, that dame you're interested in has run away from the farm where she was staying. There's a guy name of Mellish who called the hotel. He waited an hour, and when you weren't back, he told the cops. Valerie Hall decided she didn't like it at the farm any longer, and she's run out. A while before she left she made a telephone call. That's not good, is it, Colonel?"

Rollison was with Cy Day and Morris. He didn't argue his case and they didn't reproach him. Mellish had been on the telephone twice, and they knew exactly what had happened.

Valerie had seemed quite contented, but had made a telephone call unexpectedly, had gone out ostensibly to feed the fowls, and "She took my car," Tim Mellish had said. "It was found near the Highway. It looks as if she was going to meet someone there. Rolly, I can't tell you how sorry I am.

Now the three men were sitting in Morris's office in the big Police department building. There was no sound of traffic from outside; this was a rare oasis of quiet in the city and in the building. Morris had put out general calls for Valerie, and neighbouring states had been asked to cooperate; but Rollison felt as bad as a man could.

Cy Day said:

"I never did believe in fooling myself, Rolly, and it isn't going to be easy to find that girl. If Dutch is going to kill her, then we can just sit back and wait for the news that her body's been found."

Morris's expression suggested that he agreed.

Rollison said levelly: "Why did Dutch Himmy want her, in the first place? He was talking in small numbers, but that must have been to fool her. He wanted to scare her, and I can't imagine any reason except this: if she were scared, she was more likely to do what he wanted."

No one spoke.

"And if he wanted her to do something, then he'd want her alive," Rollison went on.

"Rolly," Cy Day said, "you're trying to fool yourself."

Rollison said: "Not all the way, Cy. What I've said adds up. There's another angle, too - who knew where she was?" He looked at Morris. "Did you find her?"

The policeman shook his head.

"Any of your boys, Cy?"

Day said quietly: "I knew that Morris was looking, and I was happy to leave it to him. I'm not going to make things worse by saying that you should have told us, so that we could look after her."

Rollison said bleakly: "That doesn't make it any worse, Cy.

It couldn't be any worse. But is she alive? Is Wilf?" He lit a cigarette and flicked a match out of his hand towards the window. It didn't go out when it hit the floor. He moved across the room and trod it out. "How could anyone trace her? How"

He broke off.

His expression made Day move swiftly towards him, made Morris look as if he had seen a bright light.

Rollison said, savagely:

"No one knew. If Morris and the police couldn't find her, then Dutch Himmy couldn't. She wasn't found. She"

"Rolly," Day interrupted, "you've had a rough time, you want to take it easier."

"Cy, you should let me finish," Rollison said, and went on very smoothly: "No one knew where Valerie was and she wasn't found, she telephoned someone and arranged to meet them. She gave the hiding-place away. She didn't want to go there, it was against her own judgment, and she just couldn't hold out. She believed that the one way to save her brother was to deal with Dutch Himmy, and she knew only one man who might be able to act as go-between. Call it two. Brian Conway and Mike Halloran. Didn't you say they were being watched?"

Morris was already stretching out for the telephone.

Day said swiftly: "You think she called Conway, and that he met her?"

"He met her, or he sent someone else to." Rollison was sharp; convinced.

"We've found nothing against Conway . . ."

"But plenty against Halloran," Rollison reminded him, "and here's something against Conway. He killed Al Cadey." He saw Morris's lips tighten, but the policeman didn't interrupt, just stood with the telephone at his ear. "I've been trying to work out why. Conway said that he killed Cadey because he was going to injure Valerie, but I was at the door. He could have wounded the man. He didn't, but shot him through the heart.

I've kept asking myself why and haven't had an answer, but here's an answer."

Morris had finished on the telephone.

"There's been trouble," he announced, quietly. "You coming?" He reached for his hat. "Cy, two of your operatives at the Milwest have been shot; one of my boys has, too. Sure, I had one there." They were at the door in a few strides; soon in the elevator, at the hall and spilling out to cars which were waiting. Two motor-cycle cops were already astride their machines. The engines roared. The sirens whined up and down, up and down, and the cops carved a way through the traffic as they would for visiting royalty or the President himself. They kept out of mid-town, and roared towards the Milwest Hotel.

Rollison was sitting next to Morris, in the back of the police car. Day was by the driver, looking like death.

"...and I think I know part of that answer about Conway's reasoning," Rollison said. "Cadey didn't work for Dutch Himmy any longer. Cadey knew about Wilf being missing, and he tried to squeeze for himself. That's why the play seemed so small. Dutch Himmy wouldn't be interested in a hundred thousand dollars, but Cadey would, especially if he wanted to get out of New York and out of Dutch Himmy's reach. Conway knew Cadey wouldn't go for Valerie's ear-rings the way he did if he was getting her ready for the big squeeze, later, so he guessed Cadey's game. Conway was frightened - he takes fright easily - and for his own safety he shot Cadey. Both before and after that he named Dutch Himmy, hoping that if he was caught and accused, first Valerie and then I would say he'd named the big shot, and that it would be in his favour. On the side, he hoped to impress Valerie; she could be a friend in need. He impressed her, all right - she thought he'd killed Cadey simply to save her life. She told me how guilty she felt, didn't want to believe that Conway was in the racket."

Sirens were still wailing up and down. Traffic was pulling to the right and left, to let them go.

They turned a corner, and the Milwest was in front of them.

So were other police cars. So were motor-cycle cops. So was an ambulance and a crowd of a hundred people or more. Even with the outriders, Morris couldn't get right up to the entrance.

As Rollison slid out, he saw two ambulance men coming with a stretcher between them. Morris and Day pushed a way through the crowd, and he followed. Morris went to the stretcher as it was being pushed into the ambulance. Photographers were already busy, there were pale flashes.

Morris pulled back the sheet over the dead man.

It was Conway.

Halloran, also dead, was on the second stretcher.

Cy's men and the policeman were only wounded.

"So there we have it," Cy Day said, heavily. "It's all clear now - as clear as we'll ever get it. The call from the farm was to here, the operator has a note of it. So Valerie Hall called Conway. He'd made a friend of her all right.

I don't know what deal they planned, but if Rollison's right and Conway was half-way to squealing, we can guess. Conway and Halloran would do a deal on the side, maybe to free Wilf Hall."

Morris nodded.

"You can take it that Conway and Halloran went to pick the girl up, and took her somewhere in the city," Cy went on. "Then they came back here. A man was in Conway's room, and there were two shots - that's all and it was plenty. The killer shot his way out past my men and the cop."

Rollison said: "Yes."

"Dutch Himmy meant to make quite sure that they couldn't talk," Cy Day went on. "That's his big worry."

Rollison said: "Yes."

"Listen, Rolly," Day said; "you won't help yourself or anyone by behaving as if you ought to have seen through it."

Rollison was drawing at a cigarette.

"No," he agreed. "I ought to take it easy. And why not? Russell's sister was killed because she came to see me. Valerie's walked into a holocaust because I didn't make sure that she was watched properly, because I didn't trust you or the police. Just a little mistake! But she dies."

"We don't know that he'll kill her," said Cy Day. "We don't know why he wants her, or what his game is."

"No, we don't, do we?" said Rollison. He finished the cigarette. "Has anyone talked at all?"

"Dutch Himmy's men don't talk," Cy said. "If they show any sign of talking, they get what Conway and Halloran got."

"You've checked Legs and . . ."

"Rolly," Day said, "I trust Legs as far as I trust myself, and I trust myself as far as I trust you. I can't say more. I've had Legs watching Dando; sometimes I wonder about Dando, but - let's face it, Dutch Himmy has been a name for years. He's never been caught. He is still at large because he makes sure that no one who knows him lives to tell the tale. It's ruthless and it pays off. He . . .-"

Rollison jerked his head up.

"Say that again."

"What's biting you?"

"Say it again. Why isn't Dutch Himmy caught?"

"Because he makes sure that no one who knows him lives to tell the tale."

"That's it," said Rollison, softly, and there was a new light in his eyes. "That's the beginning and the end. That's why he got Wilf. That's why he got Conway and Halloran. That's why Julie died. That's why Mark Quentin died. Remember Quentin? He died in Valerie's arms. He telephoned her. He went to the Arden-Astoria in fear of his life, to warn Valerie. Of what?"

Morris had joined them; and was watching intently.

"Whatever you're driving at," Day said, "I don't get it."

"Common denominator for death - knowing the real identity of Dutch Himmy," said Rollison. "Julie Russell - Mark Quentin - Wilf Hall - who did they know in common? Come on, tell me. Who?"

Cy Day said in a strangled voice: "No. No, I don't believe"

"Van Russell," Morris said, in a steely voice. "Van's a Dutch form, too. Van Russell. Would he kill his own sister"

"If he thought she knew him and feared she was coming to tell me," Rollison said; "wouldn't Dutch Himmy kill anyone?"

Day breathed: "Morris, let's get there as fast as . . ."

"Hold it," Rollison said, very quietly. And they waited. "Have a cordon thrown round the apartment house, but don't let Russell know we're on the way. Valerie might be alive still. First, find out whether a girl answering her description has gone to the apartment. Then let me go alone. That won't surprise Russell, won't start the shooting - but a police raid will. I might be able to fool them and get the job finished without more killing."

Morris gave his slow smile. "That could be the job for you, Mr. Rollison. I agree - Russell won't expect a visit from me or any policeman or Cy here. He won't be surprised at a visit from you. We could be wrong about Russell - and right or wrong we could use a chance to see this through without more killing. Sure you'll play it that way?"

"It's the only play possible," Rollison said.

Half an hour later, he knew for certain that a girl answering Valerie Hall's description had gone into the building with Van Russell.

The police were within call, but not too close by when a subdued Sikoski drove Rollison into the street, and stopped outside Russell's building.

"Colonel," Sikoski said, "take care of yourself."

Rollison said: "Okay, Bud."

He went forward, knowing that if he wasn't out in twenty minutes, the police would raid the building.

23

MAN ALIVE

THE Toff stepped into the hall, which looked no more impressive than before. No one was in sight. The four elevators stood at the ground floor, the doors closed. He pressed the nearer, and the doors slid open. He stepped inside. He was not watched; and it seemed unlikely that the approach to Dutch Himmy's apartment could be so easy.

First floor; second; third ... seventh.

The lift stopped and the doors slid open. Rollison stepped out. A man was doing some work on the electric lights near the lift; and it might be work which wasn't really necessary. He looked curiously at Rollison, and said:

"Hi."

"Hi," said Rollison.

He pressed the bell of Van Russell's apartment, and the clock seemed to be turned back. The first time he had done this, the door had been opened by the timid little girl, whom he hadn't known existed. She had seemed rather scared, as if overshadowed by her successful brother.

Dando had been here.

Dando.

There was no immediate answer to the ring. Rollison rang again. Then, the door opened - and Dando stood there.

Dando had always looked a fanatic, with that lean and

hungry air and the glittering eyes and the hatred and the bitterness in his voice. Now, he looked wild and savage, and the moment he saw Rollison he cried:

"Get away from here, Russell is Dutch . . ."

There was a sharp report; hardly loud enough for a bullet-shot. But it was one. Dando staggered. He backed away, coughing. His eyes flickered. Rollison swung round - but he didn't go far, for the electrician was just behind him, and he had a gun in his hand.

"Just go inside," he said; "you'll be welcome."

Rollison didn't speak.

"Very welcome, Van Russell said.

There was a gun behind and a gun in front of him; so Rollison had no choice. He went into the apartment. Dando was still coughing, and now he was leaning against a table. Russell held a gun limp by his side. He closed the door. He seemed to be alone, but wasn't, for as the door closed another man came forward, and said:

"Just raise your hands, Toff."

Rollison raised them, and felt the man slap his sides to make sure that he hadn't a gun. He lowered his arms, and Russell said with a one-sided smile:

"Well, it had to end one day."

"That's right," said Rollison. He went forward under the pressure of a gun, into the sitting-room where he had seen Dando and Russell that morning. Dando's coughing, coming from behind him, was hard and almost frightening.

It stopped.

Dando came staggering in. Rollison knew that he had a wound in his back, where Russell had shot him. He was in agony and was dying on his feet; yet Van Russell could look at him with that one-sided smile, as if he was enjoying the sight.

"Dando," he said, "why don't you take a walk?"

Dando stood by a chair. He had to hold on to it with one hand, or he would have fallen. He swayed, helplessly. Rollison moved towards him, but before he reached him, the other man said:

"Just keep still."

"The man's hurt..."

"Listen," Russell said; "we aren't interested in your humanitarianism here, Toff. He was told what he'd get if he tried to warn you, but he had to be a hero. So he's hurt. That's how he's going to stay. You're going to be hurt, too, and this time I won't make it easy; you're going to talk fast"

Rollison didn't speak.

"To - Toff," croaked Dando. "Don't - don't tell him a thing. Don't"

"Shut up," Russell said roughly.

"Val - Val's here," Dando tried to shout. "She's here! She"

Rollison cried: "What's that?" He spun round on Russell as if he was astounded, and he saw the glint of satisfaction in Russell's eyes; this was just what Russell wanted, to find out whether he had expected to find Valerie here.

The man behind Rollison said: "Take it easy."

Rollison rasped savagely: "Is that right? Is Valerie"

"That's right, and it won't make any difference to you," Russell sneered.

"Come - come see - see Russell, saw Val - saw Val come in," Dando articulated, very slowly and very carefully. "Tried - tried go for police, but"

"We can do without the life-story," Russell said. "Okay, take him away." He nodded to the man behind Rollison, who stepped to Dando's side.

Dando shouted:

"Always swore I'd kill you!" and he leapt at Russell, finding a strength which no one had thought was left in him. He actually reached Russell, his hands fastened round Russell's neck. The other man shouted: "Get away from him!" and fired into the back of Dando's head.

Dando hadn't a chance.

Rollison had.

He had a chance and he took it. He had to stall, until the

police arrived - and anything that used up time was vital. Russell believed that he could talk, so he wouldn't kill - yet.

He would only wound.

How many others were there? Where was Val? Was Wilf Hall alive? How could he best win them all a chance, as well as one for himself?

The questions flooded his mind as he leapt for the gunman, who saw him coming, swivelled round, and fired.

The bullet grazed Rollison's arm, but didn't stop him. The strength in his blow on the gunman's chin floored the man, and sent the pictures on the walls quivering.

For the first time, Rollison saw a chance of winning on his own, even before the police arrived.

Russell had Dando's dead body leaning against him.

Rollison dived forward again and grabbed the gun from the gunman's limp hand, then backed swiftly towards the door.

As he did so, another man appeared from the bedroom.

Rollison saw this man's startled expression grow into one of stupefaction, then into bewilderment as a bullet struck him in the chest, close to the heart.

He groaned as he fell.

Russell pushed Dando aside.

Rollison fired at Russell, and the bullet caught the man's gun hand. Rollison meant to kill; it was bad shooting, he simply hadn't made allowances for the fact that he was gasping for breath, and couldn't keep steady.

But Russell's gun dropped.

Rollison said thinly: "Keep away from it."

He pressed tightly against the wall. The man he had shot in the chest had fallen out of sight. Russell stood over Dando's body, breathing very hard, looking at Rollison from beneath his eyebrows. He might carry another gun, and if he did he would soon go for it.

There were sounds, as of other men in the next room.

Russell said huskily: "Don't waste your time, Rollison; there are four men in there. And they can bring more if they need them."

Rollison didn't answer.

"And don't build your hopes," Russell went on. He spoke as if with an effort; as if he was fighting against something he couldn't understand. "No one will come to help you. I've got the apartment next door both ways and the apartment underneath and on top. All the apartments in this part of the building belong to my men. And after you came up, I fixed all the lifts, and I've barricaded the only stairs. That's how thorough I am."

Rollison didn't speak.

"Lost your tongue?" Russell demanded harshly. He breathed very heavily, and kept glancing towards the door. No one could get at Rollison from the door - they might from the window, but that wouldn't be easy for any of them. He tried to imagine how they would try to get in, what Russell was waiting for.

Russell said: "Rollison, you haven't a chance."

Rollison said: "That's right," and waited. He didn't like the silence. He didn't like the way Russell stared at the door, as if he knew that help of a kind was coming for him. What would they do? And where was Valerie?

Valerie - and brother Wilf.

Russell said: "I'll say this for you, you tried to do a job, and you did it better than most would have done. You like to know something? If you'd had a little more luck you could have got away with it. You like to know something else?"

He was calmer, now.

He glanced towards the door, and grinned.

Rollison said: "All I know is that whatever happens to me or Valerie or Wilf, I'm taking you out of this world. I wouldn't let you live if it was the only chance of living myself. Don't make any mistake."

"I won't make any mistake," Russell said. "I can even believe you. I"

He broke off, grinning; as if he had seen something which really delighted him; and the way he looked put dread into

Rollison's mind. He stared towards the door, not knowing what to expect, covering Russell and determined to shoot him rather than let him go.

A man staggered into the room.

It was Wilf Hall.

24

NEWS OF WILF

THERE was no doubt; it was Wilf Hall.

He limped, badly. His right arm hung by his side, and there were dirty bandages at the elbow. There were bruises at his face, too. He hadn't shaved for days; he probably hadn't shaved since that evening when he had left the Arden-Astoria for Idlewild. His eyes were red-rimmed and glassy, from want of sleep and from pain. His fair curly hair looked matted and filthy. His mouth hung open, and he kept licking his lips.

Russell sneered: "There's your pal, Toff. Proud of him?"

Rollison didn't speak; in fact, he couldn't.

Wilf Hall looked towards him, but didn't seem to recognise him. He staggered a little further forward. For the first time, Rollison saw that there was a rope tied to his right ankle, hobbling him; and the length of rope stretched out of sight.

"There's your pal," sneered Russell, and added viciously: "Rollison, drop your gun and keep where you are, or we'll kill your pal's sister. We'll kill sweet little Valerie. You there, Valerie?"

There were other sounds of movement.

Russell shouted: "Make her talk!"

There was a pause; a gasp; a muted scream. Rollison had no doubt at all that it was Valerie, but she didn't call out.

"Make her talk!" Russell shouted wildly. It wouldn't take

much to make him lose all his self-control. "Hurry!"

Rollison called, quietly, "Valerie, don't make it worse. Are you in there?"

"Yes," she said, and her voice was pitched so low that he could only just hear it. "Yes, I'm here."

"All right?"

"They haven't - they haven't hurt me - " She paused, and then flung a word out as if defiantly: "Much!"

"We'll hurt her if you don't drop your gun, Rollison," Russell said. "You haven't a chance and nor has she. And you know what they'll do to her if you shoot me?" He leered into Rollison's face. He had looked so diffident, so pleasant, so kindly - and now he leered. "You don't know? I'll tell you. Midge!" he called.

A man said: "Take it easy, boss."

"You know what happened to the Willis girl?"

"Sure!"

"It can happen again."

"Sure, boss."

"Rollison," Russell said, "did you ever see a photograph of what happened to the Willis girl? It looked as if she'd climbed into the lion's cage at the zoo."

Here it was; the absolute climax. There wasn't a thing Rollison could do. The girl was out of sight, and all he would know about anything they did to her would be the screaming. He was sweating, and his mouth was very dry.

"Rolly," Valerie Hall called, "never mind what they say, kill Russell."

There was a sharp, slapping sound; then silence.

"Midge . . ." Russell began.

"Russell," Rollison said in an even voice, "Valerie made a lot of sense to me. If she screams again, I'll shoot you. Don't make any mistake. One more scream, and I'll shoot you first and the rest of them afterwards."

Silence.

Valerie said: "Rolly, whatever you do, don't let him escape

alive. Look what he's done to Wilf. He had him tied to a bed, he tortured him, he"

She broke off.

"Just imagine what I can do to you," Russell said viciously.

Valerie gave a little gasping sound; it wasn't a scream. Rollison didn't know for certain but he guessed that Midge had a hand over her mouth. Next moment there was a rough exclamation in a man's voice; the kind of gasp a man might make if he'd been bitten.

"He killed Mark Quentin because he could name him as Dutch Himmy," Valerie called, "and - and he thought Julie could, too. He killed Julie just in case she guessed, because she came to see you. He tried to make you talk, he told me all about that - he threatened to shoot you, and if you'd given just a hint that you thought you knew Dutch Himmy, he would have killed you and Dando." Valerie could be calm and dispassionate in spite of what was happening. "Don't let him escape, Rolly, whatever you do."

"He won't escape," said Rollison.

Wilf Hall was standing where he had been put, looking about him as if he didn't really understand what all this was about. It didn't seem possible that a man could change so much in a few days. He shuffled forward an inch or two, and then stood still again. He kept trying to turn his head to look at Valerie, but his neck was stiff; and he seemed not to have the sense to turn round.

"He's been defrauding Wilf for years," Valerie went on, "and did it under cover of other men. But Wilf began to suspect, and accused him, and Russell knew it was all over unless he stopped Wilf talking. So he kidnapped Wilf."

She stopped for breath; but only for a moment. Russell stared at the Toff and that gun, as Valerie went on gaspingly:

"He's been telling me everything; he's been boasting how clever he was. But Wilf began to suspect, and then Mark Quentin guessed, too. Russell told Mark if he went to the police, Wilf would be killed, so . . .

"Rolly, kill him!" Valerie cried.

It was easy to say.

It was easy for Valerie, with that unbending courage, to stand there and tell him what to do, for she didn't fear death for herself. But it wasn't so easy to obey. It wasn't easy to throw away his own life, on hers, or Wilfs. Rollison simply kept Russell covered. He knew that it wouldn't be long before the men in the other rooms found a way of getting in - they might come through the floor or ceiling, they might . . .

Never mind how; they'd find a way.

"Rolly, they're coming," Valerie called out, "they've got tear-gas, kill him now!"

If there was a chance to kill Russell, it was here. The tear-gas would put an end to all hope, once it was released. Kill Russell now, or throw away any chance that any of them had ever had.

"Rolly!" screamed Valerie.

He knew what he had to do.

He shot Russell in the right leg and the left arm, and dived forward towards the door. He saw Valerie, with hands tied behind her and a man at her side; he saw two others, with pistols which didn't look like ordinary automatics. He shot at them as the tear-gas billowed out. He felt it sting his nostrils. He turned and ran towards the window, shooting as he went, breaking the glass, so that anyone outside would know there was trouble here. He heard confused sounds behind him, and then something hit him at the back of his head and he just fell out of consciousness, as if death had swallowed him up.

What he didn't know was that Morris had men in the rooms across the street and that they were looking in through glasses, and getting ready to start a shooting war. He didn't know that the police were past the staircase barricade and that by the time the shooting started, Cy Day and Morris, between them, crossed the barricade and reached the landing outside the apartment as Rollison was struck a glancing blow on the head by a bullet which should have killed him.

He didn't know that they forced their way in.

In fact it was a long time before he realised that he was still alive. When he did, it was hazily; he was in a much worse state than he had been at the Belle Hotel. And he was kept in bed much longer.

Gradually, he began to get better.

He didn't know it at the time, but he first recognised people five weeks afterwards; then he recognised Cy Day and Legs Leggatt, but only vaguely. He grinned before he lapsed back into a kind of coma.

Valerie Hall was with him next time.

Then, Mary Mellish.

Soon he began to feel much better. He was able to talk. He could tell which nurses he liked and which ones he wished would stay out of the ward. He began to want to know what had happened and to ask questions. It was all rather at half pressure, he wasn't deeply interested for a long, long time.

Now, he was in a different room, pleasant and bright, overlooking the George Washington Bridge and the East River, New Jersey and, in the north, New York. It was five months after the battle in the apartment, and he knew most of what had happened now, but not everything. He knew that Russell had stood his trial as Dutch Himmy, and had been executed; that eight others had been also, and more jailed for life. He knew that Dutch Himmy had realised that there was no future in a racketeer's life, and he had planned one final kill: a big slice of the Hall fortune.

As Hall's accountant he had started well. He had planned to bring Hall stocks to a record low level, buy heavily through nominees, and take over, as an equal partner with Wilf Hall.

Wilf had discovered what he was plotting - but not until Valerie was on the way to New York.

Wilf was quickly taken prisoner. There had to be a good explanation to satisfy Valerie, and the ransom idea had been a part answer. Get Valerie worried, keep her worried, threaten to kill Wilf if she went to the police.

Cadey's double-cross had got in the way, and Conway and Halloran had fallen down on their part of the job by not spotting Rollison soon enough. What Russell hadn't realised was that Conway and Halloran wanted to get clear of Dutch Himmy, and had been waiting for a chance to fix him. Conway had known the Toff was watching, but hadn't reported soon enough.

Then, Dutch Himmy, through his man Midge, had told Conway that he suspected a double-cross; if Conway or Halloran fell down again, they would be killed. It wasn't surprising that Conway had been so jittery.

Russell was having the Milwest telephone calls reported by the operator. When Valerie had called from the village near the farm, she'd offered Conway a hundred thousand dollars if he would tell her where to find Wilf. Conway had told her that he believed he knew, had arranged to meet her - but had been killed, with Halloran, before he could leave the hotel.

Russell had met Valerie, in Conway's place.

From the beginning, his one fear had been that he had been named, as a suspect, and that the police would catch up with him. With Wilf Hall a prisoner, he had known that he would have to cash in soon; he couldn't let Wilf live. But he needed a few days to finish his frauds on the Hall Corporation - from the moment of Valerie's arrival he had been playing for time.

Nothing had gone as he planned.

First Cadey; then Conway and Halloran had made difficulties.

Then, the Toff...

From the first anxiety that Wilf or Mark Quentin had named him, he had had only one concern, which became an obsession. To find out if he had been named, and who he could trust. And he wanted to establish himself with Valerie as a loyal and trusted friend of Wilf. That was why he had tried to contact her in New York - and when his own men had proved his undoing.

He hadn't trusted Cadey, had wanted to get Valerie away from him; but Cadey had laid on the two hoodlums, whom Rollison had encountered later.

With Valerie at liberty and convinced of his, Russell's, goodwill, Russell believed he could gain the time he needed. With the Toff to reckon with, he had posed as Wilf Hall's trusted friend; but all the time he had doubted his own men, had gone as Russell to check on Conway and Halloran. The capture of the Toff and the interrogation on top of the Atyeo Building had been to try to make sure Wilf hadn't named him, and to find out exactly how much the Toff had discovered.

Wilf Hall could have saved himself the ordeal had he told the police of his suspicions of Russell. But he'd been loath to do that without proof, and his discovery that Russell was Dutch Himmy had come too late. He had tried to warn Valerie by sending a message to Mark Quentin, but Russell's man, Midge, had caught up with Quentin first.

Wilf was now in California, convalescing. The doctors said that it would be a year before he was really on his feet, but he'd been normal enough to sign a power of attorney, and Valerie was handling the affairs of the Atyeo Building and the Hall Trusts with guidance of others who were loyal to Hall.

That was all.

Rollison sat at the window of the pent-house, on a lounge chair, smoking, mildly intrigued by the mass of traffic going over the Bridge; at rush hours, it looked as if the Bridge had become alive with slugs of every imaginable size and colour, all wriggling at the same time. The evening sun glistened on the roofs and the windows, making a kaleidoscope of colour.

His cases were packed, and this was to be his last night in New York. It had cost him a lot and gained him a lot; for the Hall Trust had named his fee for him, and the figure had been almost astronomical.

It was very quiet.

He remembered that it had been quiet when he had been

at the top of the Atyeo Building.

A bell rang.

A coloured valet, who had served him since he had arrived here, walked to the front door and, a moment later, came and said: "It's Miss Val, sah."

"Oh, fine," Rollison said, and got up. He didn't think of the weeks and the months when he had been able to get up only with an effort. He felt fit and fresh, and his eyes lit up when he saw Valerie.

She looked at her glowing best.

She wore a dark blue dress of some shimmery material, and a small white hat; blue shoes trimmed with white; white gloves; as if she had just come from the best salon in New York.

Probably she had.

"Hallo, Val," he said; "you look wonderful."

"I don't feel wonderful," Valerie said; "I don't think I ever shall again when I look at you."

"Now, come..."

"Rolly," Valerie said firmly, "I've been thinking this for months, and I've decided that I shall have to say it or burst. As you're sailing for home tomorrow, it has to be now."

Rollison reached her, and put his hands on her shoulders.

"Don't burst," he pleaded. "You're much too precious."

"Fool."

"Yes, ma'am, but..."

"I insist that you keep quiet for a few minutes," ordered Valerie; and her eyes flashed, as he remembered, and she strained away from him.

"All right," he said. "Your turn."

"Rolly," said Valerie Hall with great deliberation. "I was an utter fool not to be advised by you. You were right about Brian Conway and Halloran. You were right in what you advised me to do. And you were right to tell me to stay at the farm. I was crazy. I was a self-willed, self-opinionated, half-witted little"

"Not that," broke in the Toff, urgently. "Never!"

He expected her to flare up; instead, she laughed and

relaxed a little, but went on with the same tone of deliberation.

"Well, I've got most of it off my chest. I'm desperately sorry for what I did, and it's no use talking like Cy and Captain Morris - that if I hadn't come away from the farm you might not have found Dutch Himmy and Wilf. I'm quite sure that you would have done. Quite sure. As a matter of fact, I intend to tell you exactly what I think of you."

"Val," pleaded Rollison, "don't. Be fair. And if you can't be fair, be kind."

"Rolly," said Valerie Hall, with a smile which told him much more than her words, "I think you're wonderful." She paused, and then repeated: "I think you're wonderful. I'll never be able to thank you, and nor will Wilf, but the fact remains that we agree about you. And please - is there anything we can do to say thanks. Anything?"

The Toff was so taken aback that he could only stare. Then he began to smile. Then he nodded. Then he put his hands on her shoulders again, and drew her close. Then he said:

"Yes, Val. Let me kiss you."

"Let me kiss you!" she cried.

Next morning, she was at the quayside to see him off. So was Cy Day, looking as prosperous and sleek as ever, and wholly forgiving. So was Morris, with Mary and Tim Mellish, of course, and a battery of photographers and newspapermen. In all a great crowd, and, among the party which he took on board the Queen, Sikoski with a felt hat clamping down his curly hair.

Sikoski was having himself a wonderful time.

He was going to have it even better.

He was going to London with the Toff, who had promised him the services of a London taxi every minute of every one of the thirty days he was going to stay.

JOHN CREASEY

GIDEON'S DAY

Gideon's day is a busy one. He balances family commitments with solving a series of seemingly unrelated crimes from which a plot nonetheless evolves and a mystery is solved.

One of the most senior officers within Scotland Yard, George Gideon's crime solving abilities are in the finest traditions of London's world famous police headquarters. His analytical brain and sense of fairness is respected by colleagues and villains alike.

'The finest of all Scotland Yard series' – New York Times.

GIDEON'S FIRE

Commander George Gideon of Scotland Yard has to deal successively with news of a mass murderer, a depraved maniac, and the deaths of a family in an arson attack on an old building south of the river. This leaves little time for the crisis developing at home ....

'Gideon of Scotland Yard emerges as one of the most real working detectives in modern fiction.... A sympathetic and believable professional policeman.' - New York Times

JOHN CREASEY

THE CREEPERS

"The prisoner's hand was thin and bony ... And in the centre of the palm was a pinkish mark. It was the shape of a wolf's head, mouth open, fangs showing. Although it was what he had expected to see, Inspector West felt a twinge of repugnance a stab not unrelated to fear. It was the fifth time he had seen the mark of the wolf – the mark of Lobo."

A gang of cat burglars led by Lobo cause mayhem as they terrorize the city. They must be stopped, but with little in the way of evidence the police are baffled. Just how can Inspector West manage to do this in what is a race against time before more victims succumb?

"Here is an excellent novel of law enforcement officers, harried, discouraged and desperately fatigued, moving inexorably ahead under the pressure of knowledge that they must succeed to save human lives." - Cleveland Plain-Dealer

"Furiously exciting" - Chicago Tribune

"The action is fast, continuous and exciting" - San Francisco News

JOHN CREASEY

THE HOUSE OF THE BEARS

Standing alone in the bleak Yorkshire Moors is Sir Rufus Marne's 'House of the Bears'. Dr. Palfrey is asked to journey there to examine an invalid - who has now disappeared. Moreover, Marne's daughter lies terribly injured after a fall from the minstrel's gallery which Dr. Palfrey discovers was no accident. He sets out to investigate and the results surprise even him ....

"'Palfrey' and his boys deserve to take their places among the immortals." - Western Mail

INTRODUCING THE TOFF

Whilst returning home from a cricket match at his father's country home, the Honourable Richard Rollison - alias The Toff - comes across an accident which proves to be a mystery. As he delves deeper into the matter with his usual perseverance and thoroughness , murder and suspense form the backdrop to a fast moving and exciting adventure.

'The Toff has been promoted to a place of honour among amateur detectives.' – The Times Literary Supplement